FINN'S FOLLY
Enda Maher

Finn's Folly

ENDA MAHER

SOMERVILLE PRESS

Somerville Press Ltd,
Dromore, Bantry,
Co. Cork, Ireland

© Enda Maher 2015

First published 2015

All the characters in the book are purely fictitious, and any resemblance
to actual persons, living or dead, is purely coincidental.

Designed by Jane Stark
Typeset in
seamistgraphics@gmail.com

Front cover design: David Prendergast

ISBN: 978-0-9927364-7-7

Printed and bound in Spain
by GraphyCems, Villatuerta, Navarra

For my husband PIERCE,
My children and grandchildren and for all my special friends.
Thank you for always being there for me.

Finn's Folly

PART 1

Chapter 1

'Why would anyone want to speak to anyone like that? It's unforgiveable … and rude.' Sarah was running after Jayne Jordan who was leaving the hospital as quickly as possible after an unpleasant encounter with the ward manager. She caught up with Jayne on the long corridor: 'I mean to say, telling you that you are too kind to the patients, and spend too much time with them. Lucky someone's nice to them. They wouldn't want to rely on that sour cow for a bit of compassion.'

They had reached the exit by now and Jayne, holding back tears, hugged her friend and told her to get back to work before she got the raw end of 'her self's' tongue.

Sarah agreed but before she left, suggested, 'Let's get together later and have a few drinks. I'll be off duty at six.'

Jayne looked apologetically at her friend but was anxious to go now. 'Sorry, not tonight. How about tomorrow?'

'It's him, isn't it? He's gracing you with his presence I suppose.' Sarah looked exasperated.

'Honestly Jayne, I despair of you sometimes. Will you ever get sense. He's using you …Bastard! Anyway, must go. See you tomorrow.'

The bus to Dun Laoghaire wasn't full. Sitting in the front seat upstairs, Jayne felt a sense of relief to have left the hospital and to have got away from Sarah, without too much of a telling off. They were great friends and she spoke so honestly to Jayne, it almost hurt. But … she was right, you know … that nagging inner voice kept telling her, this affair with Jack Redmond was a disaster. For two years now she had fawned over him like a puppy dog, suiting him in every way. The usual old story every time she made any demands on the relationship: 'but I'm married Jayne, I have two children. I love you but I can't leave just yet.' If it wasn't his wife, it was his kids or his career or his mother. Once he had even cited his Labrador pups as an excuse.

When the bus arrived at her stop, instead of going home to sleep, as she normally would after night duty, Jayne went for a walk on the pier. Sometimes, after a long night on duty, her mind was more alert. Probably sleep deprivation. It was a bright morning with the sun trying to break through hazy cloud. The sea was calm and calming. Jayne began to relax and, while sitting on the pier in Dun Laoghaire on that peaceful morning, as if inspired, she decided, at the age of 28, to change her life.

The house where the two Miss Finns lived was located on the outskirts of a small village in Wicklow. Miss Elizabeth Finn and Miss Edith Finn, Lizzy and Edie, had lived there all their lives. Their other sister, Dorothea, Dotty, had moved to America many years ago where she married a 'well to do' gentleman, Joseph Manning. Dotty rarely returned to Ireland over the years but her one child, Astrid, now in her 50s, had spent several childhood holidays with her aunts. She had grown very fond of Lizzy and Edie and wrote to them regularly. They loved it when they found her letters from America in the letter box.

On that same hazy, summer morning as Jayne was deciding to change her life, a letter arrived for the Miss Finns from their niece, Astrid, which would change their lives also. Sadly, they read that their sister Dotty had passed away. She had requested that her ashes be brought back to Wicklow and scattered in the garden of her childhood home. Astrid planned to arrive in Ireland the following week.

The Georgian house, where Lizzy and Edie lived, was bought by their father, Nathaniel Finn, when he returned from the war in Europe in 1945. Nathaniel was born to Irish parents in England, he was educated there and having qualified as a doctor in 1929, married his childhood sweetheart, Olivia Carr. Olivia and Nat lived happy and contented lives in a pretty village in Devon, where their three daughters, Lizzy, Edie and Dotty were born.

When the Second World War broke out, their lives, like so many others, changed enormously. Olivia moved with the children back to Ireland, while Nat joined the British Army Medical Corps and was posted to Europe. During those turbulent war years, Olivia and the three girls lived a carefree life with their grandparents in the west of Ireland. Initially, they missed their father and their life in Devon dreadfully, but as the months and years went by, they grew to love their Irish home more and more. Following VE day on 8 May 1945, Nathaniel Finn returned to his family in Ireland. Connemara had been untouched by the traumas and tragedies of the war and the family spent that summer enjoying the freedom and fun of the beaches and fields, where the girls could play from dawn till dusk with their friends and cousins.

As summer drew to its end, Nat and Olivia broke the news that the family were going to live on the east coast, in a village called Crannagh in County Wicklow. The three girls were heartbroken, their grandparents had become their second parents. Their cousins and friends were distraught when they heard the news. 'It's time for you girls to start your serious education and time for your father to set up his medical practice,' Olivia explained, although she too was bitterly upset to leave their idyllic home in the rough beauty of the west of Ireland.

'Wicklow is the most beautiful place on the east coast,' she reassured her daughters. But they sulked for days, begged and cried but had to leave. In September 1945, the family arrived in Crannagh to set up home in the beautiful house called The Folly.

It was now only three days until Astrid's much anticipated arrival from the States. Edie and Lizzy were beside themselves with excitement and also a degree of anxiety about spreading their sister's ashes.

'Where would you place the ashes, dear?' Lizzy asked Edie. Lizzy was a worrier.

'Where do you think?' Edie replied, knowing full well that Lizzy would make the decision anyway; she was not keen to waste time arguing with her.

'Perhaps we should wait until Astrid arrives and let her decide,' she added.

'That's a good idea,' said Lizzy. Edie was relieved to have the matter settled, for now anyway.

There was so much to do, Kathleen O'Hehir from the village came to help. She vacuumed, polished and washed every surface in sight and out of sight. Cobwebs that had hung happily for years from light fittings and cornices were ruthlessly destroyed and cracked crockery was relegated to the dust bin. Piles of old newspapers and magazines made a fine bonfire at the far end of the garden. The old Persian rugs which had lain for years undisturbed adorning the hall, the dining room and drawing room, were taken outdoors and beaten. The house was old and rather shabby, but now, thanks to Kathleen, was very clean.

'The garden is a bit of a shambles,' she complained to the sisters. 'Would you like Mikey to come over and tidy it up a bit for you?' Her husband Mikey was a carpenter by trade but could turn his hand to most things, if he was in the mood. He liked the Finn ladies and usually agreed to help out whenever they needed him. And so the garden too had a good makeover.

The day before Astrid arrived, the sisters roamed the house and garden congratulating themselves on how well it all looked.

'Now dear,' Edie said to Lizzy, 'let's have a glass of sherry, to toast the arrival of Astrid and poor Dotty's ashes.' They sat by the rose bed, sipping their sherry, both silently wondering what the next few weeks would bring, and how it would affect their peaceful lives.

Chapter 2

Back in the city, having thought long and hard about her problems while sitting on Dun Laoghaire pier, Jayne went home to sleep and on wakening, started to make a plan for the rest of her life. She felt an extraordinary sense of relief and freedom. The first part of her plan was very simple. She contacted the hospital, spoke to her boss and explained that she needed to take urgent leave for at least one month. Her request was not received very graciously, but the really surprising thing was, she didn't care. She had made her decision and was now determined to see it through, regardless of the consequences.

The next part of the plan was a little more difficult. Bad habits are hard to break, and Jack was a very bad habit. She composed a text message. 'Not free tonight. Have other plans. See you around. J.' No love J, no kiss. Without pause she pressed the send button and as she did, felt a dreadful lurching in her chest and thought she was going to be sick. This passed quickly and she began to feel elated. Freedom was an experience she hadn't had for a long time. As the evening passed, Jayne's resolve began to weaken. She sat on the sofa drinking cup after cup of tea, and pondered all the times she and Jack had spent together. How they met, flirted, teased and eventually after a couple of weeks, decided that love conquered all. They led a secret life, meeting whenever they could, but it was always on Jack's terms. He was married; he was busy; his life was complicated. Jayne was missing him already. She wished she hadn't sent that message. The phone rang.

She dived to answer it: 'Jack, Jack is that you?' Silence.

Then: 'No Jayne, it's Sarah.' Jayne burst into tears.

'I'm coming over now,' Sarah hung up.

She arrived shortly afterwards with a bottle of wine and a takeaway from an Indian restaurant.

'I love Rogan Josh, or whatever it's called,' Sarah remarked as she tried to open the wine. It was one of those bottles with a cork and she struggled to open it with a rather ineffective corkscrew. 'You should treat yourself to a new corkscrew, Jayne.' No answer. She poured two glasses and handed one to Jayne. She took it, but still said nothing. Sarah sat beside her friend and put her arms around her. She sobbed and sobbed. Sarah sitting quietly, gently patted her on the shoulder. An hour later after Jayne had unburdened herself, having polished off the curry and finished the wine, the girls sat together in comfortable silence.

Sarah broke the silence. 'I'm going to Wicklow next week. Will you come with me?' Her mother had asked her to collect an American visitor from the airport and drive her to her aunt's house in a place in Wicklow called Crannagh.

'Never heard of it,' Jayne interjected.

'She's my mother's friend, Astrid somebody or other,' Sarah explained. 'Mother asked me to go. I don't even know the woman so please come with me for the company.'

And so the plan was made for the trip to Crannagh.

It had been many years since Astrid last visited Crannagh. 'Oh, my! I'd almost forgotten how cute this little place is,' she exclaimed, as Sarah drove through the small village. Jayne, who had reluctantly agreed to come with Sarah sat up in the back of the car and began to take notice. It was a typical old world village; many small shops with attractive shop fronts.

'None of your big, ugly supermarkets here,' Astrid declared, obviously more than pleased that the memories of her childhood stood firm. The village stood in a valley at the foothills of the Wicklow mountains. It was a particularly pretty place with narrow streets and old buildings painted an assortment of vivid colours. The village green was beautifully kept, its flower beds a mass of seasonal blooms with benches nestling under the old chestnut trees.

They pulled up in the square and went for a stroll. 'I love this place,' Astrid enthused. Having bought fresh flowers and chocolates for Edie and Lizzy, they sat outside the village café and enjoyed freshly brewed coffee and doughnuts.

'The Tearooms is a cute name for this little coffee shop,' laughed Astrid, 'it's a pity it's too early to try out the pub. I can't wait to have a real pint of Guinness.' Sarah and Jayne smiled, thinking how typically American Astrid was. 'Let's give it a go tonight.'

The girls thought that was a great idea. Jayne was already beginning to feel much happier than she had all week and agreed with Sarah that they should book into the local hotel for a night or two. Astrid was delighted with their plan, as she knew, much and all as she loved her aunts, they wouldn't be up for any late night gallivanting.

'A few partners in crime,' she joked, 'just what I need.'

Arriving at The Folly at lunchtime the three women received a warm welcome from Edie and Lizzy who, with the help of Kathleen and Mikey, had set up the table in the shade of the old cedar tree on the lawn. They were terribly excited seeing Astrid again after such a long time. They talked for a while about Dotty and heard how she had died suddenly after a severe heart attack. Her ashes were placed with loving care on the drawing room mantelpiece.

'This was Dotty's favourite room,' they told Astrid. 'She loved to sit here with the French doors open to the garden and read or listen to music. Dotty was always so self-contained and content.'

'Well, I certainly didn't take after her,' declared Astrid. 'I can't be still for long; always making plans and doing things.'

She told them how, when her father died, she took over his business. In an unassuming way, she mentioned how successful it had remained under her watch. She was very proud of the family business and she intended to run it for a long time to come. Astrid had never married or had children, something that did not appear to bother her, except as she put it, 'I could do with an heir to the throne.'

They enjoyed lunch, smoked salmon salad, with new potatoes, followed by strawberries and cream. Conversation flowed easily. The two older ladies were enraptured with stories of life in the States. Jayne relaxed and as the afternoon wore on, she had a sense of contentment and peace that she hadn't experienced for a long time, one of belonging, of having come home. As the evening drew in with a chill in the air, Sarah and Jayne took their leave, thanking their hosts for the delightful afternoon and the delicious food and wine. Promising to meet them later, in The Village Hotel, Astrid waved them off and headed indoors to join her aunts.

'Would this be a good time to stroll in the garden and discuss a suitable spot for Dotty's ashes?' Edie enquired.

'A great idea, Aunt Edie.' Astrid loved being outdoors at this time of day as the sun began to set. It hadn't rained for several weeks, so the ground was fairly scorched and bare. The flower beds were ablaze with colour, the big oak trees throwing shadows on the lawn in the early evening light. 'The Folly is certainly a very peaceful place,' Astrid thought as they made their way to a small wooded area that bounded the south side of the property. 'When we were children, we really believed this little dell was home to the fairies. Dotty loved it here. Do you remember, Lizzy dear, how we used to creep down quietly at night, hoping to see them? It was magic.'

Edie and Lizzy looked almost sad as they reminisced about their childhood. Astrid realised this spot meant a lot to the old ladies and must have also been special to her mother, Dotty, so they agreed this was the spot for the spreading of the ashes.

Much later that night, when Astrid returned to The Folly from the village, the two ladies were asleep. Mikey had brought her to meet the girls. It was a great night out, lots of Guinness consumed in Mackey's pub, trad music and dancing.

Sarah and Jayne said they'd pop by in the morning to see how everyone was.

Astrid crept into the kitchen remembering where the medicine cupboard was, and taking a couple of paracetamol and a glass of water, hoped she wouldn't have a headache in the morning. As she made her way quietly across the hall to the staircase, she noticed Amber the family Labrador, lying in the corner. Patting him she made her way to bed. Sleep didn't come easily that night, despite having enjoyed a bit too much stout earlier. She had a lot on her mind, and was playing the scene over and over in her head: how would she break her disturbing and rather shocking news to Lizzy and Edie? She had travelled from the States completely resolved to confide her mother's secret to them as soon as she arrived in Crannagh, but having met them again after so many years, all her affection for them intensified. The thought of upsetting them disturbed her dreadfully. Eventually, still trying to figure out the best way of telling them, she dozed off.

As it happened, this worry was overtaken by the events of the following morning. Astrid awoke to a terrible crash and the sound of someone crying out in pain. She ran to the landing and was horrified when she saw her Aunt Edie lying at the bottom of the stairs in a pool of blood. She rushed down to kneel beside Edie who had tripped over Amber when she reached the last step.

'It's so unlike him to lie out here in the hall. He normally sleeps in the kitchen,' Edie said, and then winced as she tried to move.

Astrid experienced a pang of guilt. She had, she now realised, let the dog out of the kitchen last night and then closed the door on him. She felt terrible but decided this was not the time to come clean about all that. The blood, thankfully, was from a nose bleed, as Edie had fallen on her face.

Sarah and Jayne arrived on the scene soon after and warned her she would have a lot of bruising and two black eyes.

'Bad news, I'm afraid,' Jayne said as she gently examined Edie. 'You've broken your wrist.'

The local GP, Dr Mangan, advised Astrid on the phone that the nearest hospital that dealt with such injuries was in Dublin. She gave Edie some painkillers, as the doctor recommended. When Mikey arrived he drove Astrid and Edie, accompanied by Sarah, to the hospital. It was agreed that Jayne should stay behind with Lizzy, who being of a nervous disposition at the best of times, was now overwrought.

'She could have been killed,' she wailed. 'How are we going to manage? Edie does so much around the place. To be honest I rely on her completely. Oh dear! What are we going to do?'

She sobbed inconsolably. Jayne went to the cocktail cabinet, which she had noticed in the drawing room and found a bottle of brandy. She decided to take this liberty, as poor Lizzy was bordering on hysteria, if not already there. Pouring a good-sized measure into the glass, she gently held it to the old lady's lips and encouraged her to sip a drop.

'This will make you feel better, Miss Finn,' Jayne said politely.

Lizzy thanked her and sipped the drink. She took the glass from Jayne and told her to get a drop for herself. They sat together companionably, and Lizzy calmed down nicely.

Several hours later, when the ladies arrived back from the hospital, Lizzy was tucked up in bed sleeping soundly. Edie, with Jayne's help, followed suit and soon she too, propped up comfortably on her pillows, was fast asleep.

Chapter 3

How it happened that she stayed in Crannagh, Jayne was never sure. On the evening of Edie's accident, Astrid and the two girls made a light supper, opened a bottle of wine and sat talking quietly about the events of the past few days.

'I can't believe it was only yesterday morning that you girls collected me from the airport. It seems like a lifetime ago.'

Astrid shook her head slowly and looked rather worried.

'You know it was my fault that Edie fell. Amber should have been left in the kitchen. I feel so bad, as if I came here and put a curse on their peaceful lives.'

And that's not half of what's to come, she thought, but said nothing.

'We're going back to Dublin in the morning,' Sarah said. 'I'm on duty. No more time off till next week.'

Astrid thanked them for their help to her and her aunts and for their kindness when Edie fell that morning but hated the thought of them leaving.

'I feel like we are old friends already. Promise you'll keep in touch.'

Having arranged to call the next morning to say goodbye to the aunts, Sarah and Jayne went back to The Village Hotel. An early night was on the cards after a busy and demanding day. They were sleeping soundly, when they were awakened by the phone ringing. Being so unexpected, it sounded alarming in the quiet of the night. Sarah fumbled around in the dark to find it. Immediately she recognised Astrid's voice, shrill and anxious.

'It's me! Astrid!' she declared. 'Are you awake?'

19

'We are now,' Sarah mumbled.

'What did you say?' Astrid sounded puzzled.

'Oh, nothing important. What can we do for you?' Sarah regretted her tone but wanted to go back to sleep.

'Can I come over now, please? I really need to talk to you and Jayne.'

Within twenty minutes, Astrid was sitting in their room. It was 2.30 a.m.

'And so you see I really need your help.'

The conversation had taken many twists and turns, and it seemed to take a very long time to reach any conclusion. Eventually, Jayne realised she had been offered a job. At 3.30 in the morning, Astrid had made a proposal to her. Sarah was dozing in and out of sleep, reminding them that she had to go to work the next day. Jayne had wished for change, but this was all happening at a hectic pace. She didn't know what to say, and claiming exhaustion, decided she would sleep on it, and make up her mind in the morning.

Astrid also confided to her that she had some disturbing news for her aunts and would really like to talk it over, before discussing it with the old ladies.

'Please forgive me for being so pushy and disturbing your sleep,' she said to Jayne. 'I just feel so alone here and need to deal with matters quickly. I hope you understand.'

Although curious, Jayne was too sleepy to think about it now. She did wonder whether all Americans were as wired up as Astrid.

After she left, Jayne couldn't get back to sleep. Did she really want to move to Crannagh, to be nurse, carer, companion and whatever else, to two elderly ladies that she hardly knew? She would have her own accommodation at The Folly and Kathleen and Mikey O'Hehir would remain on to help. She did like the ladies, in as much as she could judge by first impressions. They seemed to be quite relaxed and happy in themselves. They both seemed fairly healthy, except of course, Edie's broken arm at the moment, but that would heal. All in all it wasn't such a bad offer. What a lovely change from the stresses of city life and of course, Jack. She fell asleep.

The following morning Astrid and Jayne were sitting in the kitchen. Sarah had dropped her off, on her way back to Dublin, promising to visit again at the weekend, and to bring some clothes from Jayne's apartment. The aunts were enjoying a lie in, with breakfast trays in their rooms.

As soon as Jayne arrived at The Folly, she told Astrid she would like to stay for a month on trial.

'If it suits everyone, we'll discuss the situation again in four weeks.'

Astrid was so relieved, she gave her a hug. She then presented an envelope to Jayne, and asked her to read the enclosed letter.

'Are you sure you want me to do that? After all, I hardly know you or your family and I'm sure this is very personal.'

'Yes, please read it, I've thought a lot about this and it will explain things to you far more easily than I ever could.'

The first letter was to Dorothea, Astrid's mother.

Dear Dorothea,

This letter will come as a surprise to you and to your sisters. My name is Louisa, I live in The United States, and I am your sister. Sorry if I have given you a shock.

My mother died recently and having told me, all my life, that although my father was a wonderful man, whom she loved very much, she would never divulge who he was. Sometimes this bothered me a lot, but I respected her wishes.

On her death, she left me a letter, telling me that it was now time for me to know my other 'real' family. I enclose that letter, so that you will understand.

Please think about all of this very carefully, and if you feel it is right, could I meet you and your family? My family.

Hoping I hear from you,

Your sister,

Louisa

The second letter was from Louisa's mother to her daughter.

My dearest Louisa,

Thank you for being a loving, caring daughter always. Also thank you for respecting my wishes all your life, to accept my word about your father. Now that I am gone, it is time for you to know the truth.

As you know, I was deployed to Europe during the war, where I worked as a nurse, caring for the injured troops. I was young, frightened and homesick. We all were. Life was tough. I met Nathaniel, your father, and fell in love with him. Our relationship was so special in those troubled times but he always explained to me how much he loved his wife, Olivia and his three daughters, who were living in Ireland during the war years. He told me how guilty he felt about our relationship, but I was happy to accept that one day, it would end. I was never going to cause harm to his family.

The war ended; Nathaniel returned to Ireland and I thought my heart would break. Never, in my youthful innocence, had I realised how devastating our separation would be. I was never going to see him again. He was, and remained for many years, the love of my life. On returning to America, I found out I was pregnant. I was shocked, and yet it somehow eased the dreadful pain of losing Nathaniel.

So you see, my darling Louisa, your father never knew about you, so you must never feel that he ignored or abandoned you in favour of his other children. I knew, being the man he was, he would have come to get us, and that would have wrecked so many lives, the lives of good people who loved him, as I did.

Please forgive me for keeping this secret all your life. Please try to understand. Now it is time for you to decide what you want to do with this information. Should you decide to meet your sisters, please tell them that their father was a wonderful man, a dedicated doctor and that he loved them. Our relationship was born out of loneliness and fear. Being surrounded by the horrors of war, our feelings knew no boundaries, not

knowing from day to day if we would survive to see the next day.
Goodbye my darling, please always carry me in your heart.
Your loving mother,
Mary Jo

There was silence. Jayne stared at Astrid, a lump in her throat, a tear running silently down her cheek.

'I know I'm being ridiculous,' she said quietly, 'but it's so sad.'

'And romantic,' Astrid replied, 'I'm not so sure that Edie and Lizzy will see it that way. That's my worry. They have never lived anywhere but here in Crannagh, and now, in their old age, that's being threatened by someone they know nothing about. It's hard to know what to do.'

'What do you mean, "threatened"?' said Jayne, looking puzzled.

'It gets worse.' Astrid was dismayed as she explained to Jayne that her mother, having met Louisa a couple of times before her sudden death, had decided she must make up to her for lost time.

'She changed her will and has left her share of The Folly to her newfound sister.' She paused and added: 'What possessed her, I'll never know. Mother was like that, always helping people and fixing things. She sometimes did it to a fault. I think this is one of those times. Oh, dear!' Astrid sat still, shaking her head slowly, lost in thought.

Later in the day when she told her aunts this news, they found it shocking, neither sad nor romantic, just shocking.

'You mean to tell me, Father had an affair? How dreadful,' Edie declared, while Lizzy sobbed.

'We're going to lose our beautiful home, probably have to go into an old people's home. I can't bear it.'

'This woman, Louisa, what is she like?' Edie asked Astrid.

'I've never met her, Aunt Edie. The first I ever heard of her was in this letter, after Mother's death. I'm sure Mother intended to tell you both all about her and sort everything out, but poor thing, she died so suddenly. She'd be devastated to think she left such a mess behind and caused you both such worry.'

The two ladies sat in bewildered silence.

Astrid decided to tell them the rest of the news now and get it over with. She suggested that first Jayne pour them all a glass of sherry.

'Brandy please, dear,' Edie interjected. 'Sherry would be no good in such a crisis.'

As they downed their brandy, Astrid dropped the next bombshell.

'Louisa is coming here next week to meet us and to see The Folly.'

'Father's Folly,' Lizzy muttered under her breath.

'Finn's Folly,' repeated Edie.

And so Finn's Folly was born.

Chapter 4

Marcus Fenton arrived at his office in the centre of Detroit city at a very early hour that morning. He liked to settle down for the day, before the phone calls started and before his secretary and colleagues were at their desks, asking him lots of questions. Marcus Fenton Associates, Architectural Services, had originally been founded by his father, Marcus Snr. He was an ambitious, arrogant man who took the company from strength to strength, capitalising on the boom years in 'the Motor Capital' of the world.

Life was difficult during the race riots of the late 1960s when the company was in its infancy, but rebuilding the city brought wealth and kudos to Marcus Snr and his co-workers. He and his wife, Louisa, lived safely and comfortably in the wealthy suburb of Grosse Point. Following the death of his father, a few years earlier, the full responsibility of the architectural firm fell on Marcus Jnr's shoulders. Along with this, came the job of looking after his mother, Louisa. She married as a young woman and never had to provide for herself or her son, so was a rather spoilt and somewhat demanding woman. None of this came easily to Marcus, who unlike either of his parents, was a quiet, self-effacing type of person. He remembered his grandmother, Mary Jo, with deep affection. Many friends and relatives compared Marcus to her, a gentle and considerate man.

This was a particularly difficult day. After a late night and having drunk a great deal, he had a headache and was anxious. Being married to Marissa had never been easy, but now it seemed like a total disaster. His marriage was falling apart in front of his eyes and it seemed that there was nothing he could do to save it. Marissa had stormed out of the house the night before, declaring an end to their seven year relationship. She was not back by morning, but what really bothered Marcus was the sense of relief he felt that she was gone. The constant confrontation had worn him down and he was now at the point of just wanting peace and quiet.

Their childlessness was at the root of the problem. Marcus knew this but Marissa had declared, early in their marriage, that she never wanted a child. Marcus longed for a happy home with lots of children. It was not to be, and was a source of continual frustration and disappointment. Here he was at 39 years of age, childless and now about to face a divorce. Knowing Marissa, as well as he did, and her self-centred, self-obsessed personality, with her absolute preoccupation with material wealth, he knew it would be a long and difficult battle. The phone ringing, startled him out of his self-pitying trance.

'Marcus, is that you? It's your mother.'

His heart sank. This was the last thing he needed, an early morning conversation with Louisa, which meant she was up to something; something that would surely involve him.

'What is it mother?' He tried to appear civil.

'You sound pretty miserable!' She went on: 'Have you been fighting with that wife of yours again? You do know, a child is what would sort you two out.'

Marcus held the phone away from his ear and let her rant on. Having had her say about him, his awful marriage, his awful wife whom she never liked anyway, and of course, his drinking habits, she eventually got to the point.

'I have to go to Ireland, Marcus. I want you to come with me.'

As usual, Louisa's request was a demand. There was no way out. Perhaps, Marcus thought, a trip to Europe was just what he needed.

'OK, mother. When are we off?'

Louisa was taken aback by Marcus's willingness to accompany her, she presumed she would have to do a bit of coaxing and manipulating.

'Next week,' she replied, feeling very pleased with herself.

When Marcus was born, in the 1970s, life for his parents was on the up and up. Business was good, money was flowing in, and they belonged to the well-off social set in Detroit. Marcus was a beautiful child with a pleasing, gentle nature which endeared him to everyone he met. He was privileged, but not in a nasty way, as Louisa and his father were far too busy making money and spending it: Marcus Snr making it and Louisa spending it! Marcus Jnr and his sister, Abigail, spent more time with their grandmother, Mary Jo, than with their parents. As a result, they learned her gentle ways, her kindness and consideration for others. Mary Jo continued her nursing career, until she retired, in her late 50s. The children loved her dearly. They grew up in a happy world, a mixture of life with their peaceful grandmother and their more hectic, wealthy parents. They had the best of both worlds. In later years, when Marcus grew into a handsome, intelligent, self-assured young man, he asked Mary Jo why his mother was so different to her. She sadly explained, how she, as a mother felt she had let her daughter down by never giving her a proper family. She had committed *the* grave sin of the early twentieth century: having a child outside wedlock. She was lucky, she said, to live in the United States, as in many other less sophisticated societies, her child would have been taken away from her.

'And so,' Mary Jo said, 'I have spent my whole life making up to your mother, for not letting her know her father and his family. I spoiled her. But she is a good, loving person, Marcus. It's just a little hard to see it sometimes.'

Abigail had left the United States soon after graduating with a degree in zoology and biology from the University of Detroit. She lived in South Africa, travelling regularly to Botswana, Malawi and other southern African countries, studying and documenting many native animal species. She was involved in making several TV documentaries. Abigail kept in touch with her mother, mostly on Skype. Louisa depended on Marcus and he was very aware of it. When his mother explained she was visiting Ireland to meet her sisters and other surviving relatives, Marcus felt a deep pang of sadness. Remembering his grandmother's great sacrifices, to prevent harm to Louisa or anyone else concerned in the unhappy affair, he worried how his mother would deal with it all and hoped, so much, that in her usual blundering way, she wouldn't cause too much upset in Ireland. He hoped to help with damage limitation. Louisa, meanwhile, delighted to have her plan in place and her beloved son on board, went ahead with her plans to travel to Crannagh the following week.

'What an adventure,' she thought. Life was always a bit of an adventure for Louisa. She was used to excitement and getting her own way.

Chapter 5

It rained in Crannagh for most of the week following Astrid's revelations to her aunts. The dark skies and heavy clouds over the mountains reflected the gloom that now pervaded The Folly. Edie was doing her best not to worry, but not Lizzy. She was sullen and sulked like a three year old, muttering under her breath, giving out about her father's errant ways and how he had left them in this unfortunate dilemma.

'It was such a long time ago, Lizzy, surely you can forget about it now. It was the war; the times that were in it,' cajoled Edie, hoping to improve the miserable atmosphere that descended on the house.

'War indeed!' Lizzy replied crossly. 'I'll give you war! Lust and adultery, that's what it was. Lust and adultery.'

Astrid and Jayne, who had been keeping very quiet, smiled at one another as they watched this normally genteel, mild-mannered lady, show no sign of weakening her resolve.

'Them's fighting words,' Jayne laughed quietly as she whispered to Astrid: 'Let's hope she mellows before next week.'

Since her arrival in Crannagh, Jayne hardly noticed the days flash by, so overwhelming was the avalanche of recent events and the rapidity with which they occurred. Now, with her elderly charges so preoccupied with the sudden appearance of Louisa in their lives, and the prospect of her imminent arrival, she turned her attention to settling into The Folly. With Astrid's help and advice, they agreed Jayne should live in one of the two guest cottages in the old stable yard.

On first impressions the cottage seemed musty and rather dingy, but within a couple of hours, all that changed. Kathleen, Astrid and Jayne, somewhat relieved to escape from the now dreary atmosphere in the main house, scrubbed, dusted, polished and vacuumed. At last, after several hours of hard work, they pulled the dust sheets off the furniture and with a sense of great pride and achievement, admired the now very pretty homestead.

'Wow!' exclaimed Astrid, 'What a beautiful cottage. I'd love to stay here myself.'

'Hands off!' laughed Jayne, surprising herself at how much she had already grown to love the little place.

Astrid disappeared into the yard and returned with a bottle of champagne. They sat around, happily discussing future plans for the cottage and the yard. Before long, the plan was hatched to reopen the second cottage. For a short time they all managed to push recent worries aside.

'I must be off now,' Kathleen said, wiping her hands on her apron and pushing her now unruly hair out of her eyes, promising she'd have Mikey there in the morning to give the place a lick of paint.

The following evening, when Mikey had finished patching up the paintwork, Jayne moved into her new home in the stable yard. It was a cobbled yard and shrubs grew randomly in old clay pots dotted here and there around the place. It wouldn't take long to tidy them up and add some colour, Jayne thought as she wandered around. Swallows dipped and dived into the long abandoned stables. They built nests in the sheltered eaves of the old buildings. Feeling happy in a strange way and liberated, her own person for the first time in years, Jayne resolved that all things being equal she would make a new start here in Crannagh.

With the excitement of the previous few days, and enjoying moving into her cottage, Jayne realised it was time to knuckle down to her new job taking care of the Finn sisters. Cooking was not her strongest point, so she decided it was time to expand her rather limited repertoire in the kitchen. The most cooking she had done up to now was when Jack had time to stay for dinner; that was rare. She remembered Jack with a jolt.

Again, she had pushed him to the back of her mind with all the recent changes in her life. She had sent him that rather curt message and had hardly given him a thought since. Thinking of him now, there were butterflies in the pit of her stomach.

'Men!' she muttered to herself. 'Nothing but trouble.'

Sarah had also slipped her mind. She was due to come down from Dublin with Jayne's clothes at the weekend but she must give her a call to fill her in on all the news.

'Where's my phone?' she murmured, rooting in her handbag. No sign of it. Then she remembered putting it on a shelf in the drawing room on that very first evening. She couldn't believe it was so long since she had used it. She used to panic if she hadn't got it with her at all times when she was in Dublin. A change for the best; definitely. Freedom. But thinking about it again, she headed into the house to look for it, to ring Sarah. Reaching the drawing room, she found Astrid standing by the mantelpiece looking upset.

'Are you OK, Astrid?' Jayne asked her. Clearly she wasn't at all OK, there were tears running down her cheeks. She wiped her eyes with the back of her hand and sniffed.

'I'm fine. Just thinking of poor old mother and all the upset she has caused, without meaning to. She was such a gentle, caring woman, wouldn't say a bad word about anyone.' She looked up at the mantelpiece where Dorothea's ashes stood in the silver urn.

'I'm afraid to mention spreading the ashes to my aunts, particularly Lizzy. She's so mad at everyone just now.'

Jayne said she'd make a pot of tea, and retrieving her phone from the shelf, headed out to the kitchen. While the kettle was boiling, she turned on her phone and found several text messages from the past few days. Sarah's message was brief and to the point: 'See you at the weekend. Hope all well. S x.' Typical Sarah. Uncomplicated and true to her word, Jayne was about to reply when she noticed three more messages, all from Jack. Again she had that sinking sensation. Although tempted not to read them, she couldn't resist. Each was much the same, asking Jayne where she was, to please answer his calls, or at least send him a message. He declared how much he missed her, how he couldn't understand why she had disappeared so suddenly, and he was miserable without her. Jayne turned off her phone and made the tea. She noticed her hands were shaking and she was getting a nagging headache. Pushing Jack out of her mind for the time being, she rejoined Astrid in the drawing room and sat in companionable silence on the sofa, enjoying the peace and quiet.

'Do you like the cottage?' Astrid enquired.

'So much. I love it,' Jayne replied with enthusiasm.

She told Astrid she was planning to plant flowers in the yard and was going to buy new curtains, bed linen, cushions and throws.

'I'd love to go with you if that's OK,' Astrid declared.

They decided to go to the nearby town next day, as the village didn't have much of a selection. Jayne enjoyed having Astrid with her, she showed great interest but wasn't bossy. Her mother died when she was young, so she enjoyed the comfortable relationship with an older, but fun woman.

'What about the ashes?' Jayne asked gently.

'Let's leave it till after Louisa's visit,' Astrid replied and Jayne had the feeling she didn't want to discuss it any further at the moment. They let the subject drop. Dorothea would remain on the mantelpiece for a while yet.

Late that evening, when the ladies had finished dinner and were tucked up in bed, Jayne sat in the cottage and reread Jack's messages. Deep down she knew she should delete them. What would Sarah say? She would be furious with her if she texted or phoned him. She put on music and started reading a new novel she found in the house. But she couldn't concentrate and kept glancing at her phone.

'Go to bed and forget about him,' her inner voice told her. She could hear Sarah in her head: 'Remember how miserable you felt when he let you down. Remember he's married. Remember he always suits himself. Remember he's a selfish bastard!'

She picked up her phone, found his name in her contacts, gazed at it for a few moments and then punched the call button.

Chapter 6

On the way home from their shopping trip, Jayne and Astrid dropped into the pub for a bite to eat. Tom Mackey's pub stood in the centre of the village and was the community meeting place. Teas, coffees, soups, fresh food and an assortment of home-made cakes and breads, were served all day, every day, as well as alcohol. The pub belonged to the family for generations. Tom and his wife Brigid brought it to a new level of excellence. The interior maintained its old world pub charm, fires blazing in winter, while in summer, outside on the street, café-style chairs and tables adorned the footpath. In what used to be a dilapidated yard there was now a beer garden, again with great attention to the flowers and trees. Old and young alike loved it.

It was mid-afternoon when Jayne and Astrid arrived and the place was quiet, the lull between lunch and evening meals. They sat inside as a nippy wind blew up. Astrid was glad to get indoors and complaining about her aching feet, she slipped her shoes off under the table.

'Does it always get this chilly in August? I've forgotten, it has been such a long time since I was here.'

'We did a lot of trudging around the shops,' Jayne remarked as she browsed the menu. 'I'm starving.'

'Me too,' replied Astrid.

A stone's throw down the street, was The Village Pharmacy. It too was a family business, passed down through the generations. The present incumbent was Patrick Fogarty, a nephew of the previous owner Pat, who never had children. It looked like the pattern was repeating itself, as Patrick, despite many dalliances, had never settled down with a woman.

Now, nearing 60 years old, his chance of marriage and children was looking less and less likely. Tom Mackey, who had known Patrick since childhood, would joke with Brigid: 'Where there's life, there's hope.'

The post office was also on the main street, next to the church. Stasia, the post mistress, always had a soft spot for Patrick at the pharmacy and was inclined to gossip. She liked bad news, a very unattractive feature in her personality in Patrick's reckoning. She had wind of the fact that something was afoot at The Folly.

'Astrid has been there now for over a week and a young woman has been employed to take care of the Miss Finns,' she confided to one of the other local gossips.

'But,' she added, dropping her voice to a suitably mysterious whisper, 'there's definitely more to it.'

Determined to find out what the story was, Stasia headed to Mackey's for tea and scones. Brigid Mackey, although curious, was not at all malicious, so when Stasia questioned her about events at The Folly, she played dumb. There had been talk around the village that 'someone' was threatening to sell the house and put the old ladies in a home. 'But,' muttered Brigid to herself, 'that's only a rumour.'

Jayne had bought lots of bits and pieces for the cottage. Brightly coloured cushions and throws, in a mixture of burnt orange and soft greens, complemented the bed linen, crisp white Egyptian cotton. Astrid insisted on footing the bill for the lot, much to Jayne's surprise and delight. Funds were short, since she had taken leave of absence from the hospital and she hadn't been paid yet for her new job at The Folly. They were chatting about these purchases and how well they'd look in the cottage when Brigid, spotting Astrid and Jayne in animated conversation, made her way over to them to take their order.

'First things first, we'll have a bottle of your best dry white wine, please Brigid, we've had a busy, tiring day.'

When Brigid returned and was pouring the wine, she enquired after the Finn ladies. 'I heard poor Miss Edie had a fall.'

Astrid assured her that Edie was doing fine but that between

Dorothea's recent death and now their other sister arriving soon with her son, from the States, the aunts were rather overwrought.

'But,' said Brigid, 'I always thought there were just the three of them.'

Astrid nodded her head solemnly. 'So did everyone else.'

Taken aback, Brigid said no more and went to get their order. Jayne, being a girl from the city where everyone minded their own business, realised for the first time how different it was in a country village. All were privy to your business. Louisa and Marcus would come as no surprise to the local people in Crannagh. Jayne made up her mind to keep all her skeletons safely tucked away in the cupboard.

Later that evening back in her cottage, feeling anxious and guilty, Jayne planned her meeting with Jack. Although it was disloyal and knowing in her heart she was wrong, she knew she must keep it a secret from Sarah. Jack had done the whole 'poor me' thing. What had Jayne been thinking when she left her job, her home and, of course, most of all, him? Had she had a nervous breakdown? Had she never stopped to think of the consequences? Losing him! What was wrong with her?

'I have to say, Jayne, I am much relieved to know you have not lost your mind and abandoned our wonderful relationship,' he declared as they finished their phone call. They agreed to meet for dinner sometime fairly soon, although Jayne explained she could not make a firm arrangement until she knew what exactly was going on with her job. She was determined not to disclose any details of her new life to Jack. Avoiding his questions, she told him she would fill him in when they met. She now knew, having listened to his self-obsessed, pompous chatter that she was right to have serious reservations about their plan to meet. She knew it was a bad idea, but . . . what could she do?

Sarah arrived the next morning, with an enormous suitcase full of Jayne's clothes.

'You must think I'm going to stay here forever,' Jayne declared.

'Hope so,' was the response.

The girls planned an evening in the village and invited Astrid to join them, if she was in the mood.

'Let's meet at your place.'

Sarah was enchanted with the cottage, deciding it was her new holiday home and Jayne prepared a lamb curry for the three of them, before they went out.

'How's the cooking coming on?' Sarah enquired, knowing cookery classes were part of the plan.

'No change really; haven't found anywhere to go yet,' she replied.

'The ladies tell me my cooking is fine, but they are very tactful.'

Astrid interjected: 'Don't always put yourself down Jayne.' She noticed Jayne's lack of self-confidence and wondered what caused her to be like that. She was such a pretty, intelligent, kind girl who, as far as Astrid could tell, would turn her hand to any task.

Her aunts were delighted with Jayne and thanked Astrid on a daily basis for finding her. They were absolutely thrilled when they visited the cottage after Jayne moved in.

'My dear,' they exclaimed with obvious delight, 'you have turned it into a little palace!'

She was very proud of her cottage. The new curtains and cushions brightened up the sitting room and with the fire burning in the grate, it made a very cosy picture. They all noticed Edie and Lizzy were in better form the past few days. Lizzy refused to discuss Louisa's upcoming visit but Edie was happy to help with the plans on the quiet.

'I'm hoping after she arrives, when Lizzy realises that she's not some sort of monster, that she'll mellow and we'll all get on OK. Fingers crossed.'

In Mackey's pub later that evening Astrid broached the subject of the American visitors due to arrive the following week. Always enjoying a bit of drama, Sarah interjected: 'What if she is an obnoxious cow?'

Astrid spluttered her drink, starting to laugh. The laughter was contagious and soon the three of them were in hysterics.

'It's not really funny though, is it?' said Jayne, trying to bring a modicum of sobriety back into the conversation. But this caused them all to start again. Patrick Fogarty, the bachelor chemist was sitting at the bar and glanced over at the three women. He always admired Astrid Manning when she visited her aunts over the years and was quite surprised to see what a fine-looking woman she still was after the intervening years. He watched as they laughed and joked but decided not to disturb them just yet. Then he noticed they regained their composure and resumed what appeared to be a serious conversation.

'Oh no, Jayne, not in the house. They can't possibly stay at The Folly, with the state poor Lizzy's in already. That would surely tip her over the edge.'

Astrid was reacting to Jayne's suggestion that Louisa and her son stay in the main house during their visit.

'I suppose you're right,' Jayne replied but was reluctant to make any other suggestions. She thought Louisa might take umbrage at being boarded out when in Crannagh and hoped she'd understand. It was decided between them that the next best answer was to book them into The Village Hotel. Astrid would make the reservations the next morning.

Dorothea's ashes were weighing heavily on Astrid's mind and she was pleased when Jayne, in her usual diplomatic way, suggested they could have the spreading of the ashes during Louisa's visit.

'It may help to break the ice with the ladies and make Louisa feel more included.'

Another decision made. The plan was to have the ceremony in the garden the following Saturday afternoon. Sarah, now a definite part of the team, was invited and happily accepted.

'Try keeping me away now that I can stay in that cottage. I love it! Of course I love you guys too,' she joked. The girls offered to prepare a meal for the occasion.

'It sounds too good to be true,' Astrid declared. She was really happy that a plan was now in place.

'Whatever happens after that is in the lap of the gods.'

'Or Louisa's lap,' Jayne retorted nervously.

Jack was again pushed to the back of her mind, she'd worry about him when things settled down at The Folly.

Chapter 7

On the morning of Louisa's arrival there was lots of activity at The Folly. Lizzy continued to act as though nothing was happening. Edie, on the other hand, was determined to make an effort for everyone's sake. She had, with Jayne's help, donned one of her now seldom worn, good silk dresses and had her hair freshly set. During the previous few days she asked the local motor mechanic, Joe, who always looked after the family's old Daimler, to come to the house and give it an overhaul. It was in great shape, according to Joe, and well up to the trip to Dublin airport. Mikey was the designated driver. Normally happy to help the Finn ladies in any way he could, his heart was not in this mission.

'Some upstart and her son arriving from America, throwing their weight around, upsetting the ladies! It's not good enough! Poor Miss Lizzy is beside herself with worry. It will be the death of her,' he complained to Kathleen, who was far too busy with the household chores to listen to Mikey 'mitering on'.

'She's probably a grand woman; after all, she is their sister, so she can't be all bad,' Kathleen added as she scrubbed the timber dining table in the kitchen.

'Get off with you now Mikey and drive Miss Edie and Astrid to Dublin, and no more of your old "carry on".'

Having a cup of tea at Mackey's before he collected his passengers, Mikey continued his rant to Brigid and Tom.

'No good can come of all this; those Yanks should stay in America and leave us here, well enough alone. I'm surprised they don't want me to wear a chauffeur's cap with all the fuss. I've even polished the car till its gleaming. You could see yourself in it. God knows what they'll have me doing on Saturday for the spreading of Miss Dotty's ashes. She's been spared all this anguish, but to be honest, I think in a way, she caused it.'

Finishing his tea, Mikey went on his way, but his conversation was noticed by Stasia, sitting quietly in the corner booth sipping tea and taking it all in. She headed up the street to the pharmacy, and under the pretence of collecting a prescription for her migraine, struck up a conversation with Patrick, filling him in on all the goings-on at The Folly.

'It's really none of our business,' he said to Stasia, grasping the opportunity to put the old gossip in her place. He did however take heed of the mention of the spreading of Dorothea's ashes and thought he might just pay his respects to Astrid and her aunts.

'Have you ever been to Ireland before, Marcus?' Louisa asked as they made their way towards the arrivals hall in Dublin Airport. Without waiting for a reply, she said she really hoped that the country wasn't as backward as she had heard it was.

'For God's sake, Mother, be quiet; we haven't even gone through passport control yet! And no, I haven't been here before.' Probably won't be allowed back either if she keeps this up, Marcus thought as he marched along beside Louisa, wondering what had possessed him to make this trip with her.

'Could you try to be a little more sensitive while we're here, Mother.'

As they stood at baggage reclaim, Marcus looked at her and thought what a pity it was that she always barged at everything and everyone without thinking. She was a good-looking woman for her age with a neat figure and ash blond, perfectly styled hair, framing a face that belied her 67 years. Helped along by cosmetic surgery, she looked not a day older than 50. If only she had the personality to go along with the good looks. Marcus had always been told that the Irish are far more aware of temperament than physical appearance.

'I hope we'll get things sorted here quickly, so we can go home again soon,' Louisa remarked, startling Marcus out of his daydream.

'What's with the "we", Mother? I certainly didn't come here to sort anything out, as you so crudely put it. I thought we were here to unite a family. "Sorting things out" doesn't sound very unifying!'

Louisa looked disgusted.

'Really Marcus, I don't know if it's jet lag, or bad manners, but I find you very disagreeable today. Of course I've got to sort things out, with or without your help. That house is partly mine and now I intend to claim it.'

The journey to Wicklow passed without incident, as having greeted Astrid and Edie fairly curtly, Louisa fell asleep. Mikey, whom she more or less ignored, other than ordering him to be careful with her very expensive luggage, thought she was not one to mess with. Secretly, he smiled to himself, thinking of Kathleen's reaction to her. Marcus was charming, and having given the two ladies a polite kiss on each cheek, he shook hands warmly with Mikey and asked him could he travel up front on the way home. Mikey, delighted with a bit of attention, waxed lyrical about cars all the way to Crannagh.

On wakening that morning, just as dawn broke, Lizzy had a heavy heart. For days now, ever since Louisa's existence was revealed, she put on a brave, if stubborn face. But in her heart she was really worried and unhappy. The Folly meant so much to her and to Edie. They had spent their lives here, since they were young girls and now she felt it was under threat, at risk. When Edie and Astrid left for Dublin, she wandered down to the drawing room. A small part of her felt guilty for not going with them to welcome Louisa and her son. She just couldn't bring herself to go. Perhaps she could make a better effort today to be more civil. Jayne and Kathleen were busy preparing lunch. Today, like the day of Astrid's arrival which now seemed like two lifetimes ago, was warm and sunny. Lunch was planned for the garden. Mikey set up the tables and chairs on the lawn before he left. Anyone who didn't know what was going on would have thought it made a very happy setting for a family lunch.

Standing by the mantelpiece, looking out the French doors at the two women busying themselves with the preparations, Lizzy felt an overwhelming sadness. After days of holding back her feelings, she started to cry. 'Oh Dotty,' she said, laying her hand on the silver urn, 'have you any idea what a can of worms you've opened?'

Meanwhile, in the kitchen, Jayne and Kathleen were preparing a feast, roast leg of Wicklow lamb with crispy roast potatoes and vegetables, served with Kathleen's delicious gravy. Jayne had collected cooking apples from the old Bramley tree in the garden and made an apple crumble.

'That could do with a bit of custard,' Kathleen remarked. Jayne had to admit she had no idea how to make custard. With Kathleen's help, she made her first pot.

'Mm, that's delicious. We'll make a proper chef out of you yet.'

Jayne was delighted. She had booked a place at a local cookery school attached to a restaurant, just outside the village. She was due to start the following Tuesday night. She wasn't that keen on the idea but felt one night a week would be manageable.

When everything seemed to be under control in the kitchen, Jayne went in search of Lizzy. She brought breakfast to her room earlier but there was no sign of her now. She headed for the drawing room and quietly opened the door to find poor Lizzy, head bent by the mantelpiece, sobbing softly. Jayne, imagining she had intruded on a private moment, withdrew, closing the door gently behind her.

'Is that you, Jayne?' Lizzy had noticed her. 'Please come and sit with me.'

An hour passed with Lizzy and Jayne in quiet conversation. They got to know each other better that day than at any other time. Lizzy confided to Jayne she was delighted she had agreed to stay to help take care of Edie and her. Edie was the younger and stronger of the two, but recently she knew it had all become too much for her. She showed great interest when Jayne told her about the cookery classes. She then reminisced about the lovely dinner parties they had hosted at The Folly, the tennis parties followed by supper and dancing in the large, now seldom used, dining room. She smiled wistfully as the memories flooded back, relaxing her and making her look far less stressed.

'You must wonder, dear,' she said, 'why Edie and I never married. If the truth be told, we never met anyone we liked well enough.' She laughed and for a flash, a beauty was revealed that had been hidden by the passage of time. Looking back years later, Jayne believed that it was the poignancy of that moment that had helped her to make her mind up to stay at The Folly.

Having welcomed their guests on their arrival from the airport, lunch was served and it was very enjoyable. All concerned were on their best behaviour, acknowledging how much effort Kathleen and Jayne had put into it. Marcus, seated next to Jayne, was very impressed.

'You're a very good cook, Jayne,' he remarked, making her blush, as she quickly explained that it was all down to Kathleen; she was only the helper.

'Actually, I'm going to cookery classes next week,' she said. 'Perhaps I could use you as a guinea pig for my new dishes.'

'You're on,' Marcus replied enthusiastically. Jayne blushed again, thinking she had been a little forward.

Later, when she confided to Kathleen that she thought she had been a bit pushy, Kathleen dismissed her concern: 'You were only being friendly, and let me tell you girl, a bit of friendliness is what's needed around here now.' She sighed and added reluctantly: 'I wouldn't trust that Louisa as far as I'd throw her. She's got something up her sleeve, I can smell it a mile away.'

Mikey, busy helping with the cleaning up, smiled to himself, thinking: 'I knew Kathleen would get the measure of that one. The cheek of her calling us 'the kitchen staff'. Full of notions, she is. Needs putting in her place.'

After lunch, Marcus suggested they all go to The Village Hotel for drinks. Louisa didn't look too pleased, but said nothing. She had been looking forward to getting away from them all, to having a bit of time to herself.

The hotel was fairly quiet at that time of the afternoon. Patrick Fogarty was having lunch at the bar, as he did most days.

'That's the bachelor life for you,' he always remarked. Seeing the little brigade arriving from The Folly, he made his way over to greet them and to offer his sympathy to Astrid and her aunts on the death of Dorothea.

'I believe you are having a memorial event at The Folly on Saturday,' he said to Astrid. 'Would it be presumptuous of me to attend, or is it strictly a family affair?'

'That is so nice of you, Patrick!' Astrid replied. 'We would be delighted and honoured to have you attend. Do you think anyone else from the village would like to come?'

And so, the small family affair grew in numbers, as lots of the locals, when invited, were happy to accept. Jayne realised she and Sarah needed to get to work with the catering. there were only three days to go. Luckily, Sarah was due a few days off work, so she would arrive the next day. 'I'll go to Marks and Spencer and pick up lots of food on the way.' Sarah was always ready to help. She was really generous and loved a good party.

'Maybe it's rude to call it a party,' she said to Jayne. 'Let's call it a wake.

'What in heaven's name is a wake?' Louisa exclaimed when she and Marcus were alone later that evening discussing the day's events. 'A wake? I told you the people here would be peculiar.'

'It's just another name for a party when someone dies,' Marcus explained, trying to keep the edginess out of his voice. All day he had walked on eggshells, wondering what his mother would come out with next. He had had a lovely day, really liking his Irish relatives and of course, their friends.

'It seems rude to me to have a party when someone dies,' replied Louisa.

'Whatever you say, Mother.' Marcus had no more energy to spare for bantering. Jet lag had caught up on them. Deciding to have an early night, they parted company, Marcus hoping to be rested and restored for whatever the next day should bring.

Chapter 8

When Astrid was 12 years old and in high school in Boston, close to where she lived a disaster beyond measure occurred. A random gun attack in the school parking lot by a senior pupil, left 12 people dead. The parents of one pupil, Simon Clarke, came to collect him that day after school before heading off to spend the weekend at their cottage in the mountains. Both parents and his twin sisters, were shot dead, along with two young teachers and six pupils. Life had changed forever.

Simon and Astrid had been friends since infant class. They lived in the same neighbourhood and their families often got together for picnics and outings. The tragedy was so enormous it took all those involved several years to even start dealing with the fall out. The media attention was constant and despite counselling, the children found it difficult to resume normal life. Simon became silent and withdrawn and Astrid was the only person he related to in any way. With the help of social workers and psychologists, it was decided the best place for Simon to be was with the Mannings, close to Astrid. George and Dorothea were more than happy to have him, to try in some way to help him to recover from his dreadful loss.

With passing time, Simon began to come out of himself but slowly. The children were lucky that both Dorothea and George were extremely kind, caring people who encouraged them both in all their talents. Astrid was a natural student whose studies caused her no problems. Simon on the other hand had a short attention span and his talents were certainly more apparent on the sports field where he excelled. His school work was steady enough but when it came to school reports, it was Astrid who shone. The two of them loved playing tennis and Simon coached Astrid to be a strong and competitive player. They rose through the ranks in their local club and when they were 16 won the Boston Open Junior League.

This victory opened up a lot of competition opportunities for the young pair. They spent many weekends travelling to venues away from home. It was during one of these trips that something began to change between them, and it was with a sense of shock and disbelief that they realised they loved one another. Playing doubles tennis was their passion and the congratulatory kiss, holding the trophy aloft with their arms around each other, now took on a new meaning. Because of their circumstances, since the death of Simon's family a lot of people, especially sports reporters, mistakenly thought they were brother and sister. What for any other young couple would have been a simple romance, for them would have raised all sorts of questions and cause embarrassment to George and Dorothea. Because of these complications, Simon and Astrid kept their relationship a secret.

This situation continued for years. During college years it became less complicated as they were both away from home. However, the old anxieties arose when Simon reached the age of 23. Holding her gently as they lay together in Simon's bed he confided to Astrid: 'This situation is wrong, all wrong for both of us and especially wrong for your parents. They are really my parents too. I wouldn't hurt them for the world.'

'What are you saying, Simon?' Astrid, sitting bolt upright, staring at him in astonishment, was aghast. 'Are you saying we have to finish with one another?'

That was exactly what Simon was saying and it broke Astrid's heart. Her devastation worsened when Simon went on to say he had enlisted in the Marine Corps. His record in sports achievements, together with his steady, if average academic reports, had helped him make the grade. He left the following week and within 9 months was deployed to the Lebanon. A year later, two truck bombs exploded in the US Embassy complex in Beirut and Simon Clarke was reported 'missing in action'.

Astrid never shared her secret with anyone. She grieved alone, lost interest in her life generally, and avoided any romantic liaisons. Simon was gone, she might as well be dead too. It was at that time that George and Dorothea, distraught about Simon's disappearance, were now worried beyond belief about Astrid.

'A trip to Ireland might help,' George and Dotty agreed and persuaded Astrid to visit her aunts. The next few weeks in the peace and tranquility of Crannagh, helped her enormously to recover, but Simon was forever in her heart.

Now, twenty-five years later, here she was again. She had in the intervening years, worked with her father in the family business. Since his death, she had been the CEO of the company, Manning Business Management Co. (MBM). The company found suitable small businesses for investors. Astrid had the privilege of travelling to many interesting locations as a result of her job. Boutique hotels, specialist restaurants, holiday villages were their specialty. Now fortunately, she herself could draw a good salary from MBM, while employing others to do the ground work. Astrid always had the final say, however, before signing off on any deal.

For some reason, Louisa's arrival with Marcus had churned up all the old memories of her last visit to her aunts. Louisa's secret had been uncovered. Marcus was no longer a secret. Secret! Secrets! She supposed everyone had them. Since she met Jayne, she sensed that she was hiding something too.

Astrid decided it was time to get to the bottom of a few things. There were two more days before the wake, the girls were busy with the preparations and Marcus had taken the old ladies out for the day in the Daimler. He was thrilled when they gave him use of the old car, for the duration of his visit.

'That Marcus is a grand fellow,' Mikey declared to Kathleen, 'the old girls have fallen for his charms, no doubt about it.'

'Wish we could say the same about the mother!' Kathleen replied, throwing her eyes up to heaven. 'That one means trouble. I can sense it.'

Mikey looked at his wife sadly, 'You certainly have it in for her. I hope you're wrong, and she won't turn out to be so bad.'

Kathleen stopped what she was doing, and wringing her hands in her apron, as she was prone to do when annoyed or worried, said to Mikey: 'I wouldn't hold my breath, if I were you.'

Chapter 9

Meanwhile, Astrid contacted Louisa to take her out for the day. 'It will give us a chance to get to know each other better.' Louisa seemed pleased with the invitation and was dressed and ready when Astrid called for her at The Village Hotel. They drove into the mountains on a beautiful afternoon. Following heavy rainfall during the night, the countryside looked washed and lush. In Glendalough, they went for a walk and chatted companionably.

'What do you think of this country, Astrid? I find it a bit strange myself. Marcus says I judge things too rashly and don't give things a chance. What do you think?'

Astrid, although enjoying the walk and chat, was very wary when answering; she felt Louisa was trying to get her on side. Perhaps she was being suspicious and a bit harsh.

'I have always loved Ireland. I've been coming to Crannagh since I was a child. The two old ladies are such dears; poor Lizzy is getting quite fragile.'

They walked on in silence for a few minutes, lost in their own thoughts, enjoying the wonderful view. Louisa broke the silence. 'That's the problem, you see, I was never given the chance to know Ireland, or you or my aunts. I was an outcast! I never even had a father. I feel so hurt, so damaged, so ….'

To Astrid's shock and dismay, Louisa started to cry, tears running down her face, sobbing. Astrid, guiding her to a rock, put her arm around her and held her close. She actually felt sorry for her. This same harsh woman perhaps had a soft side to her after all.

Sitting in the sunshine a little longer, Louisa had pulled herself together and the two women made their way back to the car park. They headed to the local pub for some food. Although it was a sunny day, the usual August, autumnal chill was in the early evening air, especially here, high in the Wicklow hills. The pub was cosy, with open fires welcoming hikers in from the mountains. The ladies decided to have homemade vegetable soup and brown bread. They sipped a glass of wine while waiting for the soup.

'Feeling better now?' Astrid enquired. Louisa shrugged her shoulders and drank her wine, but still looked miserable. Would this day ever end, Astrid wondered. This woman is hard work.

'I guess I'll never feel better until I get what's due to me. No one can give me back a family I never knew or a father I never had, but I will have what is rightfully mine. Make no mistake about that, Astrid.'

An awkward silence followed, interrupted only by Louisa's quiet sobbing. Astrid didn't go near her this time, thinking she was indulging in self-pity and attention seeking. The soup arrived and the moment passed.

'Mm, this smells good,' Astrid enthused, trying to overcome the awkward moment with small talk.

'Do you like the bread, Louisa? It's traditionally Irish.' No answer.

'Do you want more wine? I'll drive home.' Still no answer.

What with Louisa's snuffling and her bad manners, Astrid began to lose patience.

'What exactly is it that you do want, Louisa? You may as well spit it out.'

Louisa, turning towards Astrid in a very deliberate manner, glaring at her, eyes narrowed. 'I'll tell you exactly what I want, and what I'm going to get,' she paused to draw breath, creating a dramatic effect. 'I want to sell that old house, take my money and get the hell out of this godforsaken place as soon as possible!'

It was with a heavy heart, that Astrid arrived back to The Folly later that evening. The atmosphere between the two women in the car on the way back from Glendalough was sombre and fraught with tension. Astrid said very little. On her return she found Jayne and Sarah busy in the kitchen. Sarah had arrived earlier that day and greeted Astrid warmly with a kiss. 'What's wrong?' Sarah asked, backing off from Astrid's frosty welcome.

'I'm so sorry,' Astrid tried to explain it had been a terrible day but not wanting to tell them what had happened. She asked Louisa not to say anything until after the wake on Saturday although it was going to be difficult to keep it to herself. She excused herself, blaming a headache. The girls were not convinced. They continued with their work but knew something was not right. Kathleen, who had been busy with the housework, said: 'It's probably all down to that Louisa.'

Lizzy and Edie had a wonderful day out with Marcus. He wined and dined them while on a drive to the coast and they were utterly entranced with their new-found nephew. 'What a charming young man,' Lizzy confided to Edie on their return. They bade him farewell, planning to meet in the drawing room before dinner.

The girls were planning a menu for the wake and decided to make chicken pies, with lots of salads. These, together with the food Sarah had brought from Dublin, would make quite a feast. They had no idea how many guests to expect since Astrid had invited the whole village.

'Better have too much than too little,' Sarah said, in her usual generous way. They would set it out in the dining room which was now gleaming from top to bottom, thanks to Kathleen who was excited at the prospect of a dining room event. 'It's years since there's been a party in here.'

During dinner that evening the aunts were in good spirits after their day out with Marcus and pleased with the plans for Saturday's supper. 'My dears, I only wish you had seen us in our heyday. What parties we had in this room. Singing and dancing until all hours of the morning.'

Louisa, who sat scowling all evening, interjected: 'I thought it was a so called 'wake' not a party. We are supposed to be mourning our sister's passing, aren't we? Singing and dancing indeed! No respect!' Marcus and Astrid exchanged bewildered glances. Jayne was really upset to see poor Lizzy put down like that just when she had begun to come out of herself after several miserable days.

'The ladies are merely sharing their happy memories with us,' Jayne retorted rather crossly. Again she felt embarrassed for having spoken out and blushed slightly. Sarah gave her a reassuring nudge and Astrid smiled at her from across the table. It seemed she had said what the others were thinking. Louisa, not to be bested, especially by that young yuppie, had to have the last word.

'I certainly do not agree with having a party the day we are marking our sister's passing. Neither, I might add, do I agree with inviting every Tom, Dick and Harry from the village. Most of them, I'm sure, are nothing but riff raff.'

This proved too much for Astrid, who stood up suddenly to tell Louisa no one gave a damn what she thought. 'You are, in my opinion, a mean minded, self-centred, jealous woman. Dorothea is my mother, and with the consent of my dear, lovely aunts, I want the party.' Louisa looked shocked and fled from the room. It was rare for her not to have the last word or to be put firmly in her place.

Later that evening after Marcus had driven his mother back to the hotel and the aunts were in bed, Astrid and the girls sat together in the kitchen. They were all very disturbed by the events of the evening. Jayne, in particular, felt really bad.

'I shouldn't have interfered,' she said apologetically. 'It's just so difficult to hold your tongue sometimes; I've grown so fond of those two lovely ladies.'

Astrid reassured her, saying that she was the one who had let fly and what's more she didn't regret it. 'She had it coming. She's been nasty to us all since she arrived. She may be the ladies' half-sister, but she's none of their good qualities, that I can see.'

Sarah kicked her gently under the table. Marcus had come back after dropping his mother in the village and was standing listening to the conversation in the doorway.

'Oh, Marcus, I am so sorry. Louisa is your mother. I shouldn't have spoken about her like that.'

'Believe me, Astrid, I understand exactly what you mean. My mother or not, I have to admit her behaviour has been appalling since we arrived. If it's any help, I do apologise on her behalf.' He happily accepted a cup of tea and sat down at the kitchen table next to Astrid. Quietly she asked him: 'Could we get together in the morning for a chat? There are a couple of things I think we should discuss.' He looked strained and uncomfortable. Astrid guessed Louisa told him about their conversation earlier in the day.

'Of course. Let's have coffee in Mackey's, I'll meet you at eleven.'

Marcus gave her hand a gentle squeeze, letting Astrid know whose side he was on.

Chapter 10

The day of the wake dawned overcast and chilly. The weather forecast predicted a warmer, sunny afternoon in the east. This cheered them all up as the atmosphere was again rather glum since Astrid and Louisa's altercation. Louisa had not appeared at The Folly since that night. Marcus told the others not to worry.

'She never handles criticism very well, she's so used to getting her own way.'

When he and Astrid met for coffee the morning following the row, they both knew what Louisa intended to do. Marcus was deeply upset, telling Astrid he would not stand by and watch his mother cause such mayhem in the two old ladies' lives.

'They will have nowhere to go, will they?' he asked. 'The shock could kill them, especially Lizzy.'

Astrid agreed. She had seen a definite deterioration in Lizzy in the two weeks since she arrived.

'Edie is younger and tougher. Ever since she broke her arm, she is recovering very well. Thank goodness for Jayne.'

'Isn't she a topper?' agreed Marcus. 'She always steps in and takes the stress off them whenever anyone upsets them. They certainly are lucky to have her, but will she stay now that everything is so uncertain?'

'Well,' Astrid continued, 'at least there is some good news. Jayne told me the other night, the awful night of the row, she has made up her mind to stay. She has grown to love Crannagh and my aunts. Of course she doesn't know anything about your mother's plan. I feel it is best to let today happen and then deal with that problem. I hope you agree Marcus. We'll keep it to ourselves for a while yet, OK?'

They agreed that whatever happened they would do everything possible to help Lizzy and Edie. Astrid was greatly relieved to know she had Marcus on her side.

By early afternoon everything was in place with everyone dressed in their best attire and the dining table was spread with delicious fare. Sarah went walking early that morning and collected bunches of hydrangea, montbretia and fuchsia. Placed in large vases around the hall and drawing room they filled the house with summer colour and warmth. The French doors were open to the garden where chairs and tables had been put out around the lawn. Mr Carson, the rector and Father Frank the parish priest, were both invited and arrived ahead of the other villagers to plan the ceremony with Astrid and the two ladies. The rector was a jolly, hearty soul whereas the priest was rather dour and serious. For a while it looked as though each wanted to be the 'main man'. A compromise was reached: Mr Carson would recite the Lord's Prayer and Father Frank would recite a decade of the rosary. Astrid breathed a sigh of relief when the negotiations came to a satisfactory conclusion. She felt as if she was witnessing a world peace summit.

'Well, my dear, you must be very happy to know your mother's wishes are being fulfilled and that The Folly will be her final resting place,' Mr Carson said cheerily to Astrid. She was not at all happy knowing that quite soon The Folly would no longer belong to the Finn sisters. Getting through today had to be her priority, however, so putting a smile on her face she thanked both gentlemen for their involvement in the event.

The afternoon was busy. Astrid had no time to ponder on the possible loss of her aunt's home. Patrick Fogarty was among the first guests to arrive and gave Astrid a warm kiss on both cheeks. She was quite taken aback, as he was normally a shy fellow.

'While I have you to myself, Astrid, may I be so bold as to invite you out to dinner next week? I missed the opportunity years ago to get to know you better. I don't want to let the chance pass again.' Having made his speech he looked flushed and was almost breathless. He must have been practising for days, Astrid thought. What a day, what else can happen? She always found Patrick quite endearing, so, thanking him very much, she said she would love to go out with him. He smiled broadly and looked relieved. Astrid would never know how difficult that was.

The party including Tom Mackey and Brigid, Stasia Byrne, the postmistress, Amanda Carson the rector's wife, the local butcher and grocer, Dr Mangan and his wife Mary, and many other neighbours and friends, made their way from the drawing room to the woodland where Astrid and her aunts had chosen to spread Dotty's ashes. Just then Louisa made her appearance. She was attired totally in black, a long flowing dress with full length sleeves, a high collar hugging her throat, topped by a wide brimmed black hat, complete with veil covering her face. She made her way to the top of the procession standing next to Astrid, Edie and Lizzy, making it clear to all present that she was among the chief mourners.

'Who the hell is that?' Tom asked Patrick.

'That,' replied Patrick, in a hushed tone, 'that my friend, is trouble.'

Standing under the trees, a soft breeze blowing, the sun speckling the ground through the leaves, Dorothea's ashes were scattered on the soil of her beloved Folly. Prayers were recited and Amanda Carson in her sweet soprano voice, gave a rendition of 'All things bright and beautiful', one of Dotty's favourites. The group joined in the chorus, their voices carried on the still air creating a haunted atmosphere in the garden. Following the singing there was a peaceful silence as Astrid placed a plaque on the spot with this wording:

HERE LIE THE ASHES OF DOROTHEA FINN,

DEAR WIFE, MOTHER AND SISTER,

MAY SHE REST IN PEACE.

Following the ceremony in the woodland, the group went back to the house, talking quietly and respectfully among themselves. On the lawn outside the drawing room, they drank a toast to Dotty. Supper was served and thoroughly enjoyed by all the guests who complimented the girls on their fine cooking.

'We are very lucky to have lovely Jayne to look after us, and of course her dear friend Sarah, who is always willing to help. May God bless them.'

Edie asked the guests to charge their glasses and drink a toast to the two girls. Jayne blushed while Sarah, in her usual ebullient fashion, gave a series of little bows in mock exaggeration of her acceptance of the praise. Both girls were in truth delighted to be shown such affection, as they had grown so fond of The Folly and all its inhabitants.

Amanda Carson arranged a surprise for the aunts. A group of musicians, of whom she was part, set up their instruments in the drawing room and when the time was right, began to play. As the sun set over The Folly that night, there was a scene of contentment and happiness. The music played, the guests sang along. Mr Carson asked Lizzy to dance and her face lit up as he led her in a waltz around the room. Edie and Tom Mackey followed suit, as did Astrid and Patrick Fogarty. Jayne was delighted when Marcus asked her to dance. After the waltz he thanked her politely and kissed her cheek. She felt a surge of excitement and was surprised to find herself flattered by his attention.

Louisa was sitting on her own, not becoming involved in the event. When there was a break in the music, without preamble, she stood up, walked to the mantelpiece and called for everyone's attention. 'I have an important announcement to make.'

Marcus looked at Astrid, a stricken expression on his face. Louisa continued.

'As you are now all aware I am a sister in this family, the fourth daughter of Nathaniel Finn. Dorothea has bequeathed her share of the house to me. As I intend to return to the United States and stay there, I will not be taking up residence here.'

For a moment Edie, Astrid and Marcus were relieved but not for long. She continued: 'I want to tell you all, that The Folly will be put up for sale next week.'

With that she swung her dress dramatically as she exited the room. There was a stunned silence. The guests muttered quietly to one another and Lizzy burst into tears. Edie, putting her arms around her sister couldn't find words to comfort her. They sat together in shocked silence. Very gently and softly, the violinist began to play and the beautiful, poignant music gently broke the silence.

PART 2

Three months later

Chapter 11

On a cold November evening Jayne arrived home from her cookery class and was glad to get back to the warmth and comfort of her cottage. Later on she would call in to see Edie and Lizzy to check they were well and tell them about tonight's class. They loved hearing about the new recipes which, within a few days, Jayne would cook for them.

With the shock that Louisa delivered on the evening of the wake, Astrid and Jayne decided it would be best for the ladies to move into the second cottage in the stable yard, next to Jayne. This freed up the main house in preparation for sale. The old ladies were dreadfully upset at having to leave their home but when they saw the way that Kathleen, Mikey and the girls had done up the cottage for them it made it slightly easier.

'Besides everything else, you will be much closer to Jayne, just in case you need her in the night,' Astrid said, to add further reassurance to a not very happy situation. The ladies had grown to love their new home.

Jayne put the kettle on for tea and checked her emails. Astrid contacted her several times a week to catch up on progress at The Folly and of course, her aunts. She was surprised, and a little alarmed at tonight's message telling her Astrid was planning a trip to Crannagh for Christmas. The alarming bit was that Marcus planned to travel with her. She had written to the ladies so not to say a word, as they would enjoy getting the news first hand. Jayne loved the fact that Astrid always wrote letters to Edie and Lizzy. She knew they had no time for 'those old computer things'.

Marcus left Crannagh with Louisa the day after the wake, making it clear he totally disapproved of his mother's actions and would do everything he could to help sort out the problem. However, she was his mother, and although he was fit to kill her, it was his duty to see her back safely to the States. 'And long may she stay there,' he confided to his new-found family. He took Jayne aside to say a special goodbye, telling her that he would be back to try out her new cooking. Then he embraced them and left.

Astrid sorted out her aunts' move to their cottage and helping Kathleen and Mikey to prepare The Folly for viewing, she decided to return to the States to sort things out and then return to Crannagh as soon as possible. The aunts and Jayne missed her dreadfully, she was their mentor and adviser. Patrick Fogarty too, was sorry she had to leave although he hardly managed to meet her at all after declaring his intentions. He certainly would be happy to hear of her imminent return. Jayne was delighted with the news. As for Marcus, she wasn't quite so sure.

Against all better judgement, Jayne had reignited her affair with Jack. She presumed stupidly that agreeing to meet him once more would put an end to their relationship once and for all. Instead it led to more and more contact, lots of meetings and total involvement. Nothing had changed. Jack made a token effort initially to be more considerate but soon went back to his old ways. Jayne went back to accepting them. The next email was from the decorator, who was due to work on the house. That could wait till morning. Then one from Jack: 'Can't make it on Sat. Birthday party arranged. Have to go, Sorry! Jack. x.'

'More of the same,' thought Jayne. She felt hurt every time he did this to her but she still went back for more. Out of loyalty and a feeling of shame she told Sarah Jack was back in the picture one weekend when she was visiting. She expected an explosion of horror from her friend but instead Sarah stood staring at her in disbelief, shaking her head slowly. After what seemed like an eternity, Sarah declared in a slow, steady voice:

'You are my dear friend; I will always be here for you, but I can promise you Jayne, this will end in tears.'

The next morning Sarah's words came back to haunt her. For several days she blamed her queasy tummy on a bug but today her period was three days late and the reality started to dawn on her. With dread she looked at the pregnancy test. It was positive.

Chapter 12

Back in the USA Astrid and Marcus stayed in contact. They were busy devising a plan to save what they could of The Folly for Edie and Lizzy. By the time they travelled to Ireland in mid-December the plan would be ready to present to the ladies for their approval. Fortunately, as it turned out, there was little interest in the house and it remained on the market. There were a few possible reasons for this: the time of year, the recession but mainly it was because Louisa insisted on asking for an unrealistic price.

On the day they left The Village Hotel in Crannagh, Marcus could hardly bear to talk to his mother.

'What possessed you to do such a thing, Mother and in front of practically the whole village? I'll never understand it and you don't even need the money.'

'Marcus, how could you possibly understand how I feel about that family? They have had all the privileges all their lives. They never bothered with me.' Louisa stared at her son unapologetically. Marcus looked aghast.

'Mother, they didn't know you existed. How could they have included you? Have you lost your mind?'

No reply. Louisa continued to throw her clothes into her suitcase.

'Answer me, Mother,' exclaimed Marcus. 'What is your problem?'

Louisa stopped what she was doing and swinging around to face Marcus, she spoke in a slow monotone, staring directly into his eyes. 'I hate them for having had each other. I hate my mother for having excluded me. This is the first time that I can wield my power over this family and I intend to see it through.'

She turned back to her task of packing and continued: 'Now Marcus, I will thank you not to discuss the matter any further.' During the journey back to Detroit very few words passed between them. Although he knew his mother was selfish Marcus now saw a different side to her and it disgusted him. Returning to his apartment in Detroit Marcus was in for another shock.

'Marissa!' he mumbled in disbelief as he looked at his now empty home, cleared of everything except his few personal possessions and some fixtures she couldn't move. His belongings were dumped in a pile in the middle of the bedroom floor. She had even taken the bed. Too tired after the trauma of travelling with Louisa to deal with the mess he left the apartment and booked into a hotel.

'Is there no end to all this nonsense?' he thought as he poured himself a stiff drink and went to bed. Sleep eluded him. He started thinking of his time in Ireland and was surprised how much he had enjoyed it. He actually missed Crannagh and all the people he had met. 'They were real people,' he mused. He thought of Jayne; in fact he thought of Jayne a lot. Then he fell asleep.

The next few weeks passed quickly. There was so much to be done, including his separation and divorce and his relationship with Louisa had also been badly damaged. He contacted her now and again but rarely spent time with her. His sister, Abigail, came home from South Africa for a holiday, keeping Louisa occupied for a while and out of Marcus's hair. They never mentioned the family in Ireland again.

Towards the end of October, things were beginning to sort themselves out for Marcus. It emerged there was another man in Marissa's life, and she was anxious to bring matters to a conclusion as quickly as possible. Astrid contacted Marcus, suggesting a trip to Ireland in December, telling him of the plan she thought, with his help, might solve the dilemma in Crannagh. They would meet in Dublin, discuss the plan and drive to Wicklow. They agreed it would suit both of them to spend Christmas in Ireland.

One afternoon in October Astrid had a phone call from her PA, Clare. She sounded frantic and asked Astrid if she could make it for dinner with a client that evening. 'Honestly Clare, how often have I told you to avoid pressuring me like this. Can't you arrange it for another time?' Clare coughed to clear her throat and said hesitantly: 'But it's Magdalena, Magdalena Carlenni.'

'Oh!' Astrid calmed down.

Magdalena Carlenni was one of their biggest clients for years, an Italian American who made many fortunes in business. Her empire started with a small back room sewing business which had, in a short number of years, blossomed into a worldwide clothes design company. Her clothes were worn by the rich and famous, often featuring on the red carpet at the Oscars. She was a big name, not one to be messed with and having invested wisely, her fortune grew. She had acquired and disposed of five husbands in her 69 years, but for all her flamboyance and exotica, Astrid really liked her. 'She has a good heart, despite her wealth.' Her business dealings with MBM, Astrid's company, were largely to do with investment in rental holiday properties all over the world, but her favourite interest by her own admission, was her chain of exclusive boutique hotels. These were in unusual situations, peaceful places where people could escape from their hectic lives. Magdalena was based in Florida, had homes in Italy and St Lucia, but her favourite times were spent in one or other of her boutique hotels.

At six o' clock that evening, Astrid met Magdalena in a much acclaimed restaurant in Boston. She looked wonderfully elegant as always, having the air of a woman with total self-confidence but with a charming, unassuming manner to go with it. Having ordered cocktails, she sympathised with Astrid on her mother's recent death.

'Astrid, my dear,' she said, 'I am not a young woman. I have packed a lot into my life, and now I am tired; not sick, not sad, just tired. I want to retire and I want you to find for me, the perfect place.'

Astrid was astonished. This was a type of assignment she had not taken on before. A big ask!

'I want to live away from the high life, somewhere quiet but beautiful. Somewhere not too hot. I'm fed up with hot, busy countries and bustling cities. I think what I want is peace. Somewhere I can live quietly but have fun when I feel like making it.' She said this with a knowing grin, her eyes twinkling, the old magic still there.

'Can I rely on you Astrid? You and your father before you have never let me down; I know you won't this time either. Can I leave it with you?'

And so having enjoyed dinner, fine wine and interesting conversation, Astrid found herself going home with a very challenging, if intimidating mission to fulfil. Later that evening, she phoned Marcus. 'I have a plan,' she told him and went on to disclose her recently conceived idea. Marcus listened intently and when Astrid had finished her spiel, he was almost speechless.

'It's certainly different,' he said. 'Go for it Astrid. I'm with you all the way.'

And so it happened, that Magdalena Carlenni was invited to join Marcus and Astrid on their trip to Ireland for Christmas.

Chapter 13

Kathleen O'Hehir's niece agreed to move into Jayne's cottage for a few days to keep an eye on things while Jayne went away. 'You need a break, love,' Kathleen said kindly. 'You've been looking a little peaky recently.'

Jayne wanted so much to confide in her about her pregnancy but thought better of it. She was in a state of shock and didn't know what to do so was heading to Dublin to try to sort things out in her head. A few hours later, she was standing on Sarah's doorstep when the door burst open.

'Jayne!' Sarah exclaimed, surprised and delighted to see her. Then she noticed her rather stressed demeanour and continued: 'So what's he done this time?' She ushered Jayne into her apartment and standing very close to her, looking her directly in the eye, said: 'She's found out about you, hasn't she?'

'No,' Jayne replied, 'it's worse.'

Sarah looked alarmed. 'Worse?' Sarah exclaimed, 'how worse?'

'Much worse!' Jayne was now struggling to hold back her tears.

'Much worse? How much worse Jayne? Is he dead?' Sarah was now almost shrieking.

'No, worse than that.'

Sarah now apoplectic replied. 'Worse than dead. How can it be worse than dead?' She caught Jayne by her shoulders and made her look at her. 'Tell me, for god's sake tell me, what is wrong, Jayne.'

'I'm pregnant.' Jayne was now sobbing inconsolably.

Sarah dropped her hands and flopped into an armchair. 'Oh Jesus Christ!'

'You told me it would end in tears. I should have listened. I'm such a fool.' Jayne put her head in her hands and continued crying.

Standing up and putting her arms around her, Sarah sighed. She felt angry, angry with Jayne, angry with him.

Speaking more gently now she asked: 'What did he say about it?'

'I haven't told him.'

'Because you know how he'll be. You know he'll say all the horrible things that egotistical, selfish lovers say. He'll say, "How do you know it's mine?"'

'Sarah!' Jayne swung around, 'it's Jack we're talking about.' She was outraged.

'Exactly, Jayne. It's Jack we're talking about and believe me he will say that and more. He'll say you should get rid of it.'

Jayne was horrified and speechless. She was sure Sarah was wrong and that Jack would help her deal with her pregnancy and her new baby, when the time came.

The following evening, Jayne told Sarah she was right:

'He said everything you said, and more. He told me he couldn't possibly put his marriage, his career, his family at risk. He said it was my fault. *My fault!* OK, I forgot my pill. After I left Dublin, I was careless, because I thought I didn't need it.' The girls sat, looking at each other, neither knowing what to say next.

Jayne was sure her pregnancy would mark the end of her short but happy days in Crannagh. Lying in bed in Sarah's apartment that night, unable to sleep, she made a plan. She would not have a termination. She had always disagreed with abortion and felt she'd cope very poorly with the aftermath. She thought for a short time about adoption but quickly dismissed this also. The idea that there could be a child of hers out there, somewhere in the world, a child she would never know, an adult she would never know, was an appalling option. She would have her baby, rear it herself and hope for the best. Thinking of how she would break the news of her pregnancy to Astrid and her aunts was very disturbing. They surely wouldn't want a pregnant, single woman and then a single mother, looking after them. She decided to write a letter to Astrid, claiming she had to go back to Dublin for personal reasons. She realised there were difficult times ahead and it terrified her. She felt alone, vulnerable and extremely sad. Putting her hand on her tummy, she spoke quietly to her baby: 'Don't worry little one, we'll make it through.'

Jayne was surprised when she received a prompt reply from Astrid, almost by return of post. Astrid was horrified that Jayne was leaving.

'Are you lonely? Are the aunts difficult to look after? Have you met someone in Dublin that you want to be with?'

Questions; questions; no answers, well no answers that Jayne wanted to give Astrid, especially when she was thousands of miles away. Eventually, a compromise was reached. Jayne agreed to stay in The Folly until Astrid arrived in December. It was only a few weeks away. They would discuss it further then. 'Please Jayne, reconsider your decision. You have become very special to us all. At least spend Christmas in Crannagh and help us with our plans for The Folly.' Thinking this was a good idea that gave them all a chance to reorganise themselves, Jayne said nothing about leaving to the aunts or Kathleen O'Hehir. She would stay put till after Christmas and then who knows?

It was a harsh winter. By the end of November, the country was covered with snow. Crannagh, situated among the foothills, took on the appearance of an Alpine village. Several roads were blocked and driving was dangerous. It was quiet following the heavy snowfall, the atmosphere still and hushed. Jayne and Kathleen were busy getting ready for Astrid's return the following month. She asked them to prepare the main house for her guests. There would be no viewings while they were there over the Christmas holidays.

Edie and Lizzy, now well settled in their cottage, were particularly cosy during the snow. Jayne kept fires blazing and a pot of soup simmering on the range. Often they would sit together in the evening in one or other cottage playing cards or watching television. Mikey or

Kathleen always called by to check that all was well. The weeks passed slowly and peacefully.

When the ladies were settled at night, Jayne, now alone, would think about her future, her baby, her life. Sarah was in constant contact by phone or email but unable to visit because of the treacherous road conditions which went on for weeks and the weather showed no sign of improving. She had a large, extended family, parents, siblings, cousins, aunts and uncles and was always coming or going, to or from a wedding, a christening or a funeral. Jayne knew how close her family were and she had to admit she envied her. When she thought about her baby, she felt a terrible loneliness. This child would have only a mother, her. That frightened Jayne. What if something happened to her? There would be no one to look after the child, no grandparents, aunts or uncles. No father. She cried, not for herself, but for her unborn baby.

Jayne was used to being alone. Her father, Arthur Jordan, left her mother when she was six years old and when her mother died tragically in a traffic accident her grandmother reared her from the age of eight. She could hardly remember back to those days but had a vague memory of her grandmother arguing with her father when he came to visit. His visits became rare. By the time Jayne went to boarding school her contact with him was largely down to birthday and Christmas cards. Her father, travelled the world, working as an engineer on the oil fields. Now her grandmother suffered from Alzheimer's disease and was in a care home. Jayne visited occasionally but had grown distant over the years. Her grandmother no longer recognised her.

One evening in early December, just weeks before Astrid and Marcus were due to arrive, Jayne decided she must find her father, not just for her own sake but for her baby's sake most of all. She dug out her father's old Christmas cards, the last dating back over eight years as she never let him know when she moved house. He always put his present address and contact phone number on her cards, obviously craving a reply from his daughter. The last address she could find was in Norway. The card was dated 2006.

With a lot of emailing, writing letters, phone calls, through different contacts she eventually traced her father to what seemed to be his most recent address, luckily in Scotland. She had to decide what to do next, it was only two weeks to Christmas and Astrid was on her way. Late one night Jayne wrote a letter to her father. She posted it the next day and then began the wait. Would he reply?

Chapter 14

On the day Astrid and Marcus returned to Crannagh the excitement in The Folly was palpable. The heating was on, the beds aired, open fires blazing in the drawing room and dining room. From the kitchen where Jayne was now in charge, wafted the glorious smells of dinner cooking. Kathleen had the place gleaming from top to bottom, as were the cottages. The weather became milder after a gradual thaw but snow remained banked in sheltered corners of the stable yard and garden. The hilltops were capped with snow, the air crisp, the sun shining. It was a lovely day.

'Just like old times, eh,' Mikey remarked to Kathleen as they put the finishing touches to the Christmas tree in the hall.

'We'll turn the Christmas lights on after dinner this evening, if that suits. Mr and Mrs Finn made a tradition of that in their day, I believe. The ladies will be delighted.'

Edie and Lizzy were very happy later that evening, standing in the hall, the Christmas tree ablaze with lights, the fire burning in the now seldom used hearth, Astrid and Jayne standing next to them with Kathleen and Marcus.

'Let's hope this won't be our last Christmas in this old house,' Edie remarked. 'A toast to the Folly, and all who sail in her,' Marcus joked as they raised their glasses. Jayne excused herself, on the pretence of fixing things in the kitchen with Kathleen.

'Are you sure there's nothing wrong, pet?' Kathleen asked her when they were alone. Jayne was silent, she had kept her secret until now but somehow the burden became greater as the days went by. She hadn't heard from her father and now she was going to have to explain her imminent departure to Astrid.

'I'm pregnant Kathleen!' she blurted out. 'I'm eight weeks pregnant and I feel terrible.'

Kathleen looked taken aback, momentarily, but then, putting her arms around Jayne, said: 'That's wonderful news, Jayne, strange but wonderful!' Jayne was amazed at her reaction, expecting her to be shocked and disapproving.

'But I'm a single mother, no father. It's the wrong time for me to have a baby.'

Kathleen looked at her sadly. 'Let me tell you, pet, there's no wrong time to have a baby. Mikey and I would have sold our souls for a child. It just never happened. It wasn't to be.'

'Oh Kathleen, I'm so sorry, I never thought about that. I presumed you chose not to have children.' Jayne spoke quietly, astonished to have Kathleen reveal such a confidence to her.

'We're too old now, well I am, nearly 50, so I try not to have any regrets. We're blessed to have each other, Mikey and me. Now no more worrying. We're here for you, Jayne, and we'll help you in every way we can.'

Later that night, when Edie and Lizzy were settled and Marcus was reading in the drawing room, Jayne was again stunned, this time at Astrid's response when she told her about the pregnancy.

'Jayne, a baby in The Folly, how wonderful.'

'But I'll have to leave. You'll need someone more reliable to look after the ladies, not a single mother with a new baby.'

Astrid shook her head, hugging Jayne. 'Nonsense. Your child will add happiness to our lives. Please don't leave, be part of us and help to save The Folly.'

The next day dawned bright and sunny. Relief washed over Jayne when she remembered the support and kindness she received from Astrid and Kathleen the previous evening. She felt light hearted for the first time in weeks. Bringing breakfast to the ladies she reminded them they were all meeting in the drawing room before lunch to hear

Astrid and Marcus's news. Like Jayne, Edie and Lizzy had a great sense of well-being since Astrid returned.

'When is her friend from America arriving?' they asked Jayne.

'About three days,' she replied.

'I do hope she's a nice person, not another spanner in the works!' Lizzy was still nursing a terrible resentment towards Louisa, remembering her visit with horror.

Later in the drawing room Astrid and Marcus revealed their plan to the aunts and Jayne. Jayne felt very privileged and included in the family when Astrid invited her to attend the meeting. 'I really want you and your child to be part of this plan. I hope you like our idea and decide to stay.' Once again Jayne had a sense of having arrived; from day one she was always at home in The Folly.

Half an hour later the plan was revealed and Astrid and Marcus waited for the reaction with trepidation. It was a 'big plan', lots of changes but…!

Edie broke the silence: 'A wonderful idea. Not alone do we all stay put in our home, but it will bring great happiness to many others. What do you think, Lizzy?'

Lizzy shifting in her chair, sniffed in her disapproving way. The others held their breath waiting for the bombshell to drop. 'It will be fine, once no one tries to put us out of our cottage. No more moving around for me, I'm too old!' There was an audible sigh of relief around the room.

When Astrid first came up with the idea of buying Louisa's share of the house, she discussed the idea with Marcus. At the time Marissa had just agreed to a fairly manageable divorce, leaving Marcus with enough funds to throw in his share. Astrid was delighted. She was going to have to borrow a substantial amount but Marcus's share would reduce that. Of course they both knew acquiring the house was only the start. Refurbishment and continued maintenance were major considerations.

'That's where Magdalena comes in,' explained Astrid. She told them about her client who was looking for a property to invest in and although she had never been in Ireland before, she was convinced it was the place for her.

'Fingers crossed she'll still think that after her visit. She's arriving in three days' time. I like her, so let's hope you all do too,' continued Astrid, explaining what Magdalena had proposed as a business plan for The Folly, should she decide to invest.

'The short term plan has already been put in place, without any of us realising we were doing it,' laughed Astrid. 'Your move to the cottage was stage one, but now instead of selling the house, it is going to have a complete makeover!' She went on to say Magdalena wanted to live on the property, but planned to choose a site to build her own house. They all started to suggest possible places for this new house and their enthusiasm was encouraging but, Astrid reminded them: 'That will be up to Magdalena.'

'Oh we know that, dear, but I'm sure she'll appreciate our experience of a lifetime living here and ask for our opinion.' Lizzy was not going to sit back and say nothing. Astrid, Marcus and Jayne exchanged a wry smile. There should be fun ahead with the aunts.

Astrid explained the rest of the plan, that the main house, with Magdalena's investment, would become a 'Residential and holiday hotel for retired ladies and gentlemen', reminding them again that all this depended on Magdalena's decision whether or not to go ahead with the investment.

'Let's all have a really good Christmas holiday and hope that in January we will be going ahead with our new business.'

A few days later, just before dusk Stasia, the postmistress, was the first person to notice the arrival of Magdalena Carlenni. Her driver parked outside the post office while Magdalena popped into the newsagent. She was tall, good looking, and beautifully dressed. 'She looks expensive,' Stasia confided to her next customer. 'I wonder who she is. She headed out the road towards The Folly, one of Astrid's American friends, no doubt.'

Magdalena had made it clear to Astrid she didn't want to be collected from the airport. 'I need to get a feel for the place myself before meeting you and your family. Wanting to settle here will depend so much on my own real impression of the place.' Astrid understood what she meant. As soon as she arrived at The Folly and met everyone, it would be a holiday. Firstly she had to be alone to take it all in.

'No wonder she's such a successful woman,' Astrid remarked to Marcus, 'she takes on all her projects first hand.'

On her trip in from the airport, Magdalena saw that Dublin, like any other city was busy with a lot of traffic and some very dodgy drivers. As they approached the city centre she noticed, that unlike in the States and elsewhere, the buildings were not high rise. The spires of churches were more apparent than skyscrapers and she liked that. 'So quaint,' she remarked later when emailing home. As the car approached the Shelbourne Hotel where she was staying for a few days to acquaint herself with the capital, she was pleasantly surprised at the delightfully festive landscape that greeted her, Christmas lights everywhere and an enormous tree at the top of Grafton Street. She spent a pleasant few days at the Shelbourne where the concierge was a fount of information about Dublin, and the history of the area, as well as sharing lots of anecdotes with her about many famous guests who had 'stayed with us'. She enjoyed his friendly banter and loved how he spoke of the hotel as though it was part of his family. 'Of course madam,' he told her, 'I've worked here, man and boy, like my father before me.'

Magdalena toured the city over the next few days. She believed it was only polite to familiarise herself with her host's country. She learned facts of history, ancient and modern, visiting the art galleries, museums, colleges, government buildings, the Dáil, cathedrals. After three days, she had fallen in love with Dublin. She visited pubs and restaurants all over the city, loving the variety of food available, and as for the Guinness, it was the favourite. She came upon a trad night in

O'Donoghue's pub, a stone's throw from the hotel and was charmed by the way both staff and patrons alike were helpful and friendly.

'And tell me now, girlie, where are you off to on your travels?' an old Dubliner enquired.

'To tell you the truth, my good man,' Magdalena replied, 'I believe I'm going home.'

'Well,' he replied, 'the best of luck and may God go with you.'

And now here she was in Crannagh, what appeared like a million miles from the hustle and bustle of the city, in what seemed to Magdalena one of the cutest places she'd ever seen. The lady in the newsagent was helpful and friendly and Magdalena waved at a woman in the post office, who seemed to take an inordinate interest in her. She asked her driver to wait for a few minutes while she wandered around. At The Village Hotel she was attracted by the festive lights and peering through the window decided it was a good idea to introduce herself to the local hostelry. In she popped and ordered the ubiquitous glass of Guinness.

'You're on holiday around here?' the bar man asked.

'Just arrived. I'm staying at The Folly,' she replied.

'A lovely spot,' he said eyeing her up and down. 'Lovely ladies too, the Finn ladies.'

It was all adding up to being alright in Magdalena's book. She was now on her fourth day in Ireland and she liked it a lot. She was cautious by nature, and so kept an open mind, despite her inherent inclination to go for it. A few days at The Folly with Astrid and all the others should help her make her decision whether or not to set up home here.

As she got up to leave the young man behind the bar called over to her: 'Goodnight now. Happy Christmas.'

'Goodnight and thank you,' she replied. 'See you again.'

Kathleen was keeping an eye out for Magdalena's car so she could call Astrid to greet her. She heard the crunch of the wheels on the gravel and looking out the window saw a large black car sweep up to the front of the house. She called Astrid who threw the door open, letting the light and warmth of the house spill out into the garden in welcome. They greeted one another warmly, Magdalena kissing Astrid three times on her cheeks in the Italian way. Linking Magdalena's arm Astrid led her into the drawing room, where the ladies, Jayne and Marcus were gathered to welcome her. She was charmed by the friendliness and warmth she received, and thanked them all for inviting her for the Christmas holiday. As was their wont, they poured the champagne and Marcus proposed a toast: 'Welcome, Magdalena. I hope you'll be very happy here with us. Now let the party begin.'

Two nights later, in the early hours of St Stephen's Day, The Folly was burned to the ground.

Chapter 15

The tragedy of the fire at The Folly in the small village of Crannagh was carried for several days on the national news. It was an unexplained tragic accident in which two people had lost their lives. Being Christmas time, with all the festive trees and lights it was presumed the cause was an electrical fault or due to the risks associated with open fires and candles.

Magdalena, who suffered from insomnia, left the house in the early hours of St Stephen's Day. Muffled up in her warm coat, scarf and gloves she headed out to wander around the area. Time slipped by and before she knew, it was dawn. Marcus enjoyed Christmas Day, and imbibed lots of wine. When everyone retired for the night he decided to call on Jayne suggesting a night cap. They chatted for quite a while and when Marcus fell asleep on the sofa, rather than disturb him, Jayne threw a rug over him and went to bed. Edie and Lizzy had retired early after a long and enjoyable day. They slept soundly in their cottage. Astrid perished in the fire.

Kathleen returned to the house later on Christmas night to check everything was alright and had started to clean the dishes which had piled up over the day. She made herself a cup of tea, sat back on the rocking chair and fell asleep. She too died that night. The enormity of the tragedy and the terrible grief of losing Astrid and Kathleen left the household reeling. Edie and Lizzy were so overwhelmed with events that Jayne called Dr Mangan.

'Edie is strong,' he told Jayne. 'It will take a long time for her to recover but I worry that Lizzy has lost heart and possibly her will to live. That can happen to old people when the going gets too tough.'

Jayne, helped by Marcus, took great care of the two ladies and as the days went by they began to get a little better.

Astrid and Kathleen were buried on the same day and the whole village turned out. Mikey was distraught but told them when he was up to it he would come back to help them. Marcus and Magdalena were at a loss as to the best thing for them to do. In the space of a week Magdalena loved everything about Ireland and especially Crannagh but decided to go back to Dublin for a few weeks to give everyone time to recover to some degree. Before leaving, she called Marcus aside for a quiet word.

'Marcus,' she said in her accented way, 'do you believe there is any future now for our plans for The Folly? Would it seem dreadfully insensitive to suggest restoration of the old house after the shocking tragedy that has occurred?'

She was very distressed herself after the fire as on returning from her walk that morning she came upon the most awful scene. From a distance it looked like an amazing dawn, the sky ablaze but as she drew near the house, she realised it was not a natural phenomenon. Clouds of black smoke rose into the air, sparks like fireworks shot upwards from the house. She was terrified and realising that it was way out of control ran to the cottages to raise the alarm. After that everything became hysterical, a vague memory of fear, helplessness and dismay. As the fire tenders arrived along with ambulances and police cars Jayne, Marcus and Magdalena, looked on in terror. The ladies, despite the turmoil, remained asleep in their cottage probably exhausted after the long Christmas Day which they had thoroughly enjoyed. However, eventually with the aid of the Gardaí, Jayne and Marcus wakened them and brought them outside to safety. They were horrified and terrified calling for Astrid. Magdalena looking back now felt their hearts would break.

Having thought it all through, Marcus and Magdalena decided that they would keep in touch while Magdalena was in Dublin. Marcus planned to stay on in Crannagh at least until everything was sorted out legally.

'When time passes and the grief has lessened, we'll talk again about the plans.' They both agreed.

It turned out that Astrid with her usual efficiency had left her share of The Folly to Marcus which meant that now he, along with Edie and Lizzy, were co-owners. The weeks following the fire passed as though in a dream. Jayne, while taking care of Edie and Lizzy felt as if the world had gone into a different orbit. With Astrid and Kathleen gone she felt alone and was pleased that Marcus decided to stay in Crannagh for a while. She had waited patiently for several weeks to hear from her father. Now, in the middle of January, she began to give up hope of ever seeing him again. Her pregnancy was going well except for the occasional bout of nausea. Now that Kathleen was dead, the only other person who knew about her pregnancy was Sarah and she had moved to England for six months to train in midwifery. 'Don't worry, Jayne, I promise I'll be back in time for the baby's birth.' Jayne was almost alarmed at the mention of the birth, the reality of a real, live baby was still like a mystery to her. But it was going to happen and she needed to make plans.

The stable yard was close to the main house but luckily at this sad time there was no direct view. The acrid smell of smoke lingered in the air for weeks. Edie and Lizzy couldn't bring themselves to go and look at the burnt out shell of what had been their home since childhood. They missed Astrid dreadfully. Having no children of their own, Astrid was their closest relative. Whenever they took the ladies out Jayne and Marcus used the back avenue to avoid the sad vision of the main house. The more Jayne got to know Marcus and the more time she spent with him, the more she liked and trusted him.

'He is a very kind man,' she reported to Sarah.

'That makes a change,' Sarah replied, having a dig at Jayne about her previous relationship with Jack.

'You should tell him about the baby, really you should Jayne. Then at least you would have someone to talk to. It's not good to have all that pent up inside you. You need to share your feelings. It's awful being so far away.'

Jayne was shocked. 'How could I tell him about my baby? He'd be horrified, probably never speak to me again.'

'Look here Jayne,' Sarah retorted harshly. 'If he really is your friend he won't react like that. He may be surprised but he won't turn against you. Don't be daft.' As usual Sarah was, in her own inimitable way, talking a lot of sense and Jayne knew it.

Marcus too was somewhat bewildered having found himself in this most unlikely situation… alone in Ireland, responsible for two elderly ladies whom he hardly knew but had grown inordinately fond of over the past months. His mother was constantly contacting him, wanting him to return to the States. 'It is beyond me, what you are doing in that godforsaken place, Marcus. Your place is here with your family. What are you thinking staying there for so long?'

'My family?' thought Marcus, 'A mother for whom he now had little affection since her behaviour in Crannagh.' In fact he believed she was somewhat responsible for a lot of what happened. Life would have pottered along as always for the Finn ladies, if she hadn't caused all that upset; Astrid would be back in Boston; Kathleen would probably have been at home in her own house on Christmas night and poor Magdalena wouldn't have endured the dreadful trauma of the fire. As for Jayne, she was often in his thoughts and he realised she was largely the reason he was still in Ireland. 'Oh Jayne,' he said to himself, 'you've got me, I'm smitten.' There was a lot to do, a lot of plans to make, so Marcus pushed thoughts of Jayne to the back of his head.

During the next few months while life was settling into some sort of normality in The Folly, Marcus and Magdalena were in constant contact, Marcus travelling regularly to Dublin to meet her. There was some good news, a little light at the end of the dark tunnel. The insurance company investigating the fire accepted it was an accident caused by an electrical fault and agreed to meet the claim in full. This news was welcomed by Edie and Lizzy, as otherwise they stood to lose everything. This also meant it was time to move ahead with the business plan.

'Do you think the time is right to discuss it?' Magdalena asked Marcus. They were sitting in the Shelbourne Hotel where Magdalena had based herself following the fire. The staff were surprised to see her return so soon but hearing of the dreadful events at Crannagh everyone in the hotel went out of their way to make her welcome.

'Perhaps it would be a good idea to invite Edie and Lizzy to stay here in Dublin for a little while. The break would do them good and we can discuss the plans at our leisure.'

Magdalena organised a suite for them and left it to Marcus to arrange the trip.

At first Lizzy was doubtful about leaving Crannagh, even for a short time but Edie who loved the idea finally persuaded her to go.

'Afternoon tea in the drawing room overlooking St Stephen's Green, was the winning point,' Marcus told Jayne over supper later that evening. 'We'll leave the day after tomorrow if you can be organised. Will you be OK here on your own while we're in Dublin?'

Jayne assured him that a little while alone was probably what she really needed.

'You must be stressed by all that's happened since you arrived,' Marcus remarked, showing his concern for her. 'You were bound to feel it all very badly since you became so attached to Astrid and Kathleen. And then you had all the worry of the aunts and their grief.' He patted her gently on the arm as he spoke and to her horror Jayne felt tears pricking her eyes.

'Don't cry now, you idiot,' she thought and pulling herself together she shrugged and laughed telling Marcus she was a 'tough old cookie'.

'I doubt that,' he replied but let it pass.

Two days later Edie and Lizzy arrived in Dublin and were delighted to see Magdalena as they moved into their suite and settled down to enjoy their stay. Within a couple of days having discussed all the plans, they all agreed it was time to restore the old house and continue with plans to develop the residential and holiday hotel at The Folly.

Magdalena suggested that if he agreed, Marcus should oversee the design and building of the hotel and Magdalena's new house. Restoring the old house would need to be done with great sensitivity and Marcus was more than happy to accept the job straight away. 'It's time to celebrate this great plan so what do you say to another week or so here in Dublin?' Edie and Lizzy were delighted to accept Magdalena's invitation. A few days later Marcus headed back to Crannagh.

Chapter 16

On the same afternoon in mid-March that Marcus left Dublin to return to Crannagh, Arthur Jordan, Jayne's father, arrived home to Edinburgh after an extended stay in Canada. He left Scotland in early December for Nova Scotia to spend Christmas and the New Year with his children. They had grown up travelling around the world with him but both of them, twins, a boy and a girl, fell in love with Canada. When their father returned to Scotland they decided to stay put. Arthur was very close to his younger children, having reared them singlehandedly after his partner Victoria, their mother, left when they were very young. He made the terrible mistake of losing contact with his eldest child following the breakdown of his marriage and he was determined that would not happen again.

He had a pleasant trip and arrived back in good spirits to his apartment, the top floor flat of an old Georgian house in one of the more desirable areas of Edinburgh. He was relieved to find everything safe and sound. Katy, from the flat on the lower floor, kept an eye on things when Arthur was away and gave him a warm welcome. She was an art student, 20 something years old and full of fun.

'Well, Granddad,' she exclaimed, 'nearly time you came back.'

'Nice to see you too, kiddo.' Arthur gave her a peck on the cheek.

'What's been happening around here since I left?'

'Not a lot to be honest. Mrs Peter's cat died. He was pretty old anyway, bit like herself. I went home for Christmas and Hogmanay, lovely but very cold in the mountains. We went skiing, nearly froze to death. Oh by the way, I left all your post on the kitchen table, mostly

Christmas cards I'd say. You'll probably want to dump them now, a bit unseasonal. Must go, see you later.' And away she breezed the same way she had arrived. Arthur smiled thinking how good it was to have some young blood around the place. He missed the twins dreadfully when he left them. At 22 they were full of life, crazy dreams and ambitions. He loved that, it kept him young.

While making coffee, he picked up the bundle of post and glanced through it. Lots of cards as Katy said; might as well just dump the lot. Then again that seemed rude, considering the trouble people had gone to, sending them in the first place. The least he could do was have a look at them. He opened one or two and confirming they were greeting cards, he threw them back on the table deciding to look at them later.

Arthur spent his life working on oilfields around the world and was now retired. In contrast to his previous life when he travelled a lot, living in all sorts of strange and some exotic places, he was now a home bird and the only reason he left Edinburgh was to visit his children. At 65 he was fairly contented. He had a good pension, a nice home and he loved living in Scotland. He considered retiring back to Ireland but always a certain sadness and guilt stopped him. After he left his first wife, having met and fallen head over heels for Victoria, he never expected to lose his small daughter. But, as life transpired, when his wife died and little Jayne was left alone with her grandmother, it became more and more difficult to see her and spend time with her. He could understand that his mother-in-law was angry and hurt, but despite his pleading with her, she kept his daughter from him, making contact so difficult that it eventually broke down. Now he didn't know where she was, how she was, who she was with. If he let himself think about her, it broke his heart. He had never had a serious relationship since the twins' mother left. He devoted his free time to them when they were growing up and as a result was now very close to them. But there would always be that empty space in his heart. The twins were aware they had an older sister, and every now and again, would suggest to Arthur that they should search for her. They never had any success.

Arthur was a tall, good looking man. His thick hair was now silver, his skin dark, tanned all year, after all the time spent in hot climates. He was fit and well. Women loved him, but other than an occasional dalliance, he wasn't very interested anymore. In reality, Arthur Jordan was an extremely self-contained, easy-going man who enjoyed good food, good wine and a game of golf, an occasional swim and lots of books. It took a lot to disturb his day-to-day routine. However, three days after his return from Canada, when he decided it was time to tidy his flat, he was overwhelmed on opening another envelope to see it was a letter from Jayne. He actually began to tremble and was shocked at his own reaction, when reading her words, tears ran down his face. She had included her address, phone number, and directions to her home, 'should you wish to visit'. He was horrified to see the date on the letter: 14 Nov. It was now mid-March. Four months! Four whole months! He was so afraid that she'd have changed her mind about seeing him, or have moved address again, that he was unable to bring himself to phone her. He would travel to Ireland right away and meet his daughter face to face. He booked a flight to Dublin for the next day, planning to travel to this village called Crannagh, in Wicklow, where Jayne hopefully still lived. He would decide what was best when he arrived. He also made a reservation in the local hotel, hoping he could suss out where Jayne lived and take it from there.

A mixture of excitement and anxiety prevented him sleeping that night and combined with the jet lag he was experiencing from the Canadian flight, made him feel almost giddy on the morning of his departure. He took the same suitcase he brought from Canada, as he had no idea how long he'd stay. Katy met him in the hallway as he was leaving for the airport and was astounded to see him, complete with suitcase, dashing out the front door. 'What the hell are you doing? Where are you off to now?'

'Ireland!' Arthur replied 'To visit my daughter! Will explain when I get back.'

'Cheers so, Granddad! Love you!' said Katy, none the wiser.

'Love you too, kiddo!' And he was gone.

Meanwhile in Ireland, Marcus was excited on his way back to Crannagh from one of his meetings in Dublin with Magdalena. The plans they had made for the restoration job were all set and he was thinking he'd stay in Wicklow for the foreseeable future. He couldn't wait to see Jayne and tell her all the news.

He phoned her from the car and asked her to meet him for lunch: 'I've lots to tell you.'

'Where are the ladies?' she enquired, and was amused to hear they had settled nicely into the Shelbourne Hotel and intended staying on with Magdalena for a holiday.

'We'll never keep up the standards they'll expect when they come home,' she joked.

Marcus laughed, 'I'm going back to the hotel to freshen up and then I'll be out to collect you.'

He was staying at The Village Hotel since the fire and two hours later, Jayne and he were enjoying lunch in the hotel dining room, while Marcus filled her in on all the developments. She was thrilled to hear how happy Edie and Lizzy were with the plans for The Folly.

'What about the cottages? Will they be involved in the reconstruction?' Jayne asked, wondering if she and Edie and Lizzy would have to move again. The plan was, Marcus explained, that the stable yard would be left as it was, except that two more cottages would be developed.

'It will make a lovely little settlement of its own and you and the ladies will not be disturbed at all. Of course we can organise some improvements during the building, so keep an open mind on any changes you'd like.'

Jayne thought for a moment, considering how perhaps, the cottage could be better adapted for her baby.

'A penny for them,' Marcus remarked smiling.

'Oh, nothing. Just daydreaming,' replied Jayne.

On that same day, Arthur landed in Dublin Airport and hired a car to drive to Wicklow. He began to relax as he left the city behind and headed into the peaceful countryside. The rain and cloud cleared and the day was bright and cold, seasonal for March. Having spent so many years in oppressively hot climates Arthur enjoyed the crisp, cold weather. The sun shone as he drove through the Glen o' the Downs. It was reminiscent of years ago, what seemed now like a lifetime ago, a lifetime that included Jayne. Thinking about his daughter, he smiled to himself, as he could feel her coming closer to him with every mile. When he eventually arrived in Crannagh, having made several unintended detours, he was more than pleasantly surprised at the quaintness of the village.

'Definitely a hidden gem,' he thought as he looked around for a parking space. A car park on the south side of the village kept the streets relatively traffic free, adding to the old world charm. Despite the chilly wind, a couple of resilient souls sat chatting on the village green, well wrapped up in coats, hats and scarves. They greeted Arthur as he made his way toward the post office, having decided that would be the best place to enquire about the whereabouts of The Folly. Seeing him enter the shop, Stasia immediately dropped what she was doing to give him her undivided attention.

'Good morning, sir. How might I help you?' She spoke to him with that usual curious tone in her voice, which really meant: 'Who are you and what are you doing here?'

Arthur, although he had been away from Ireland for a long time, remembered to beware the village gossip.

'Good morning, madam,' he replied politely. 'Could you please direct me to The Folly?'

Stasia, shaking her head slowly and meaningfully, looked at him with a tragic expression and hesitantly asked: 'Haven't you heard?'

'Heard what?'

'About the fire!' she solemnly replied.

'What fire? When?' A chill crept over Arthur as he became impatient with this dramatic woman

'Can you please tell me what you are talking about.'

'Oh dear, you obviously haven't heard. The fire at Christmas, burned The Folly to the ground. Two women, may God bless their souls, died! Very tragic!'

Stasia was at her melodramatic best. Arthur was weak and sick as he rushed from the post office. He looked this way and that up and down the village street and spotting the Garda station, headed straight to it. Garda O'Brien was in the office and came to the customer window promptly. Seeing the state that Arthur was in he came from behind the counter and sat him down on a bench.

'What is it, sir? What happened to you?' he enquired gently.

'The Folly,' Arthur asked stuttering. 'Who died in the fire in The Folly? Please tell me!'

Arthur was almost ashamed at the relief he felt when Garda O'Brien told him: 'Miss Astrid and poor Kathleen O'Hehir, who worked there, perished on the night of that dreadful disaster.'

Arthur sat with his face in his hands, tears of relief now flowing. Pulling himself together, he thanked the Garda and assuring him he was now alright, he went back out into the fresh air. He didn't notice Stasia, standing by the post office door, taking in all that was happening.

Arriving at The Village Hotel, he sat in the foyer before checking in and began to gather his wits after the fright he had got, hearing about the fire. Several people came and went while he sat there including a young woman with a good-looking American man who walked out of the dining room chatting companionably as they paid their bill. He heard the young man say: 'Thank you; I would love to come for supper this evening.'

They left the hotel and Arthur went to the desk to check in. What he needed now was a good sleep. He'd decide what to do later on when he was rested.

It was mid-afternoon when Marcus dropped Jayne home after lunch that day. 'See you at about eight o'clock then?' Marcus called as he drove away. He told her over lunch how much he was looking forward to her long-promised cooking. He had of course eaten with Jayne on many occasions, but always in company. Tonight, he hoped would be special. He really wanted to tell her how he felt about her.

Jayne, meanwhile, busied herself clearing up the cottage. She had taken advantage of the ladies' absence to spring clean both cottages and it was at the stage where everything was all over the place. 'Never mind,' she thought, 'he'll probably not notice.' Quickly she tidied up the sitting room, dining room and kitchen and set about making supper. As she worked she thought how close she had come to telling Marcus about her pregnancy. When he suggested making changes to the cottage she almost blurted it out, telling him that would be a great help. Abandoning the stove, she strolled around the cottage, dreaming of having a playroom, a nursery, a utility room. It would make such a difference when her baby arrived. Now that Astrid and Kathleen were no longer with them she dearly hoped that the others would welcome the new arrival. She realised she was beginning to show a proper bump so could not keep her secret much longer. She was very much alone, especially since Sarah had left for London, but she believed Marcus was a good friend. She had become quite attached to him over the past few months. Remembering supper, she headed back to the kitchen. Perhaps it was time to confide in Marcus. 'Perhaps tonight,' she thought.

Chapter 17

It was fairly busy in The Village Hotel that evening. Marcus went to the bar at about seven o'clock before heading out to the cottage for supper. He was looking for a bit of Dutch courage, it was a long time since he was in this situation. Telling a young woman how he felt about her made him feel nervous; perhaps she would laugh at him or worse still, take offence, and give him his marching orders. 'Well,' he said to himself, 'I'll go for it and hope for the best!' There was something about Jayne that just melted his heart. She was beautiful but not in a contrived way, natural, with a slight shyness that made her seem vulnerable, but not needy. She was independent. In fact, Marcus thought she was very alone in the world. She never spoke of family, only once briefly mentioning her father while chatting, something about having lost contact with him, but she quickly changed the subject when he tried to pursue the matter. He did know that her mother died when she was a child and she was reared by her maternal grandmother. 'But,' he thought, 'there is something mysterious about her and that makes her even more interesting.'

He was deep in these thoughts when he felt a tap on his shoulder. It was Stasia from the post office. 'I do hope I'm not disturbing you,' she said in a half whisper. Marcus turned to speak to her, but had no intention of engaging in a long conversation as he knew she was a gossip. She, no doubt, was talking to him just to be nosey and get some information about The Folly.

'Good evening, Stasia,' he said politely. 'Is there something I can do for you?'

She took a deep and meaningful breath and looking furtively over her shoulder said, again in a low secretive voice, which was really annoying Marcus: 'Do you see that man sitting over in the corner, reading the newspaper, grey hair, tanned?'

Marcus glanced in the direction she indicated. 'Yes, Stasia, I see him; now what about him? I've never seen him before,' Marcus answered impatiently, wondering what in the name of God this man had to do with him.

'Well,' Stasia continued, 'he was in the post office today, enquiring about The Folly and he was very upset and ran out the door when I told him about the fire.'

Marcus was a little curious now but didn't want to encourage Stasia to stay longer, so he shrugged his shoulders saying:

'Perhaps he knows the Finn ladies. Anyway it has nothing to do with me. Now I must be off. Goodbye Stasia.'

She was disappointed he wasn't more interested and give her more information about this stranger.

After she left Marcus looked over at the man again wondering should he say something to him. Maybe he was here to visit or perhaps it was to do with the proposed business at The Folly. It was nearly 7.30 p.m. so he'd have to make up his mind quickly or he'd be late for supper. He decided there was nothing to lose and wandered over to the corner table. By way of introduction, he held his hand out to the gentleman seated at the table.

'Hello, my name is Marcus Fenton. You don't know me but I believe you were enquiring about The Folly earlier today. I thought I might be able to help you.'

The man stood up and shook Marcus's hand with a strong, friendly handshake. 'Thank you,' he said. 'You are connected to the Folly then?' Marcus went on to explain he was part owner of the property, not giving away too much information as the stranger had not introduced himself. Eventually he asked him what his business was with The Folly.

'I do apologise,' he said. 'My name is Arthur Jordan, and I believe my daughter, Jayne, may be living there.'

Marcus was so taken aback with this news that he sat down at the table and declared he needed another drink.

'Me too,' Arthur said, apparently relieved to have unburdened himself. While they had their drinks, Marcus told Arthur that Jayne was safe and well and living in the cottage.

'In fact I'm going to visit her now. Why don't you come with me?'

They decided it would be best for Arthur to arrive at Jayne's cottage alone. She would get a surprise and no doubt a shock.

'I'll follow you up there in another hour or so, when you've had some time together.'

Arthur thanked him profusely for his help and understanding and agreed to the plan. 'You must be a very special friend to Jayne,' he said as he got up to leave.

'I hope so,' Marcus replied with feeling. 'See you later.'

Chapter 18

When Arthur arrived at the cottage on that fateful evening, Jayne threw the door open, expecting to see Marcus.

'Oh, hello, sorry, I was expecting somebody else. Can I help you?'

Arthur was almost speechless, seeing his daughter for the first time in years, so long that they didn't recognise each other. He wanted to take her in his arms and hug her forever, however he was an intelligent man, and knew this was a very delicate situation. Jayne sensed his discomfiture and became uneasy.

'What do you want?' she asked nervously. Arthur knew he had to say something. He wished he'd planned it better. This was the most difficult moment of his whole life.

'I'm your father,' he blurted out and they stood staring at each other in disbelief. Thinking about it now, Jayne found it hard to remember the sequence of events after that. Arthur asked if he could come in and she stood aside to let him pass. Once inside the cottage, having stared in disbelief for another few seconds, she gave him a hug and a kiss on the cheek. He was surprised and delighted that she hadn't rejected him.

'I can't believe you're actually here', was all she could say over and over again. They talked freely, she asking how he had found her and him laughing, saying: 'You sent me your address.'

'But that was months ago. I had given up hope of finding you. I'm so happy.' And she hugged him again.

Arthur spoke to her gently. 'I have a lot of explaining to do, you have a lot of forgiving to do.'

'I know, I know. We have so much to sort out. But tonight let's just be happy and celebrate being together again. How long can you stay in Ireland?' she asked.

'For as long as it takes,' he assured her.

'Oh my goodness,' she exclaimed, 'Marcus is coming to supper. He's a good friend. In the excitement, I forgot all about him.'

'He's on his way,' Arthur told her.

'What?' she was more than surprised that Arthur knew this. Just then, Marcus knocked on the door.

After greeting each other they spent many hours that evening talking until Marcus said: 'I should go, and let you guys have some time on your own. I'll call by tomorrow and see how you are, Jayne.' He was disappointed he hadn't been able to tell Jayne how he felt about her, but he knew now was not the time. Any more surprises would definitely lead to emotional overload.

'Wait. Please wait a minute. There's something I have to tell you both and now seems like the right time. I can't keep it to myself any longer. I'm pregnant!'

Arthur's response was amusement. 'Good God, girl, have you no mercy on your old father? Here I am in Ireland to meet my long lost daughter and now I hear I'm also meeting my first grandchild. Amazing! Things just keep getting better.'

He never asked her about the father or any other details, just wanted to know that she was well and when the baby was due. Marcus looked dumbfounded. He couldn't believe she kept this secret for so long. Jayne explained that Astrid and Kathleen knew and were very kind and understanding.

'But all that time since the fire, you've kept it a secret. You could have told me, Jayne. I really do understand and will help you all I can.'

Jayne's main problem now, was to convince the two of them that she was not delicate or sick, just pregnant. She now knew she need have no fear of lack of care and support.

Two days later, Jayne was travelling to Dublin with Arthur and Marcus. It all seemed so unreal she had to pinch herself to realise it was not a dream. When Marcus phoned Magdalena and the Finn sisters to tell them the news about everything that happened in their absence, Magdalena invited them to join her, Edie and Lizzy, for a short stay in Dublin.

'We have so much to hear about and so much to plan, it would be just amazing to spend some time together here, away from everything. Also, I can't wait to meet Jayne's father. It's all so thrilling. She must be so happy.'

She was really happy.

'You're very quiet there in the back,' Marcus turned briefly to look at Jayne. She had been completely in a world of her own, remembering the past few days.

'We'll be in the city shortly. Are you OK?' He glanced at her in the rear view mirror.

'I'm just fine, thanks.' In fact she couldn't have been happier. Her father was sitting directly in front of her and there was a comforting warmth looking at the back of his head, listening to the timbre of his voice. She was still amazed he had come to find her.

They arrived at the Shelbourne Hotel and the next few hours were busy and filled with excitement. They got a great welcome from Magdalena and the ladies, who proudly showed them the run of the place. 'We'll leave you to settle yourselves in, and perhaps we'll meet for dinner later?'

The next week passed in a whirl of activity. Magdalena and Marcus, with Edie and Lizzy's approval, met with bankers, engineers and planners to set the plan for The Folly in motion. It all sounded amazing but Jayne was far too distracted by Arthur's presence to take much of it in. 'It's not that I'm not interested,' she explained to the others, 'it's just hard to process it all.'

They reassured her she needn't worry about any of it, except Marcus reminded her, the renovations for her own cottage. She was very pleased about that and knew Arthur would advise her.

The Finn sisters heard of the baby on the evening that Jayne arrived. Edie did her best not to look overly surprised. Lizzy almost choked on her food but covered up by saying she had a 'little bit of a sore throat'. Magdalena was delighted, saying that a new baby was always good news and remarked it would bring luck to The Folly, in its resurrection from the ashes.

'Remember,' she said, 'new house, new baby. It's hardly likely any of the rest of us women could oblige.' This caused great amusement, and Jayne was deeply grateful to Magdalena for helping the awkward moment to pass. She, like Edie and Marcus, knew that Lizzy would come around to the idea, in her own time.

The next day Edie and Lizzy took afternoon tea in the drawing room, as they did every day since arriving at the Shelbourne.

'Can you believe that Jayne is expecting a baby?' Lizzy whispered to Edie.

'Not at all respectable, is it,' she sniffed disapprovingly.

'To be honest, Lizzy,' Edie replied, 'it's a shock, or maybe I should say, a surprise. But having said that, it's the times we live in. We really must support her in every way possible; she is so caring to us. It's the least we can do.' Lizzy didn't look convinced.

The weather in Dublin for the time of year, was very pleasant, fairly dry, occasional showers, and a light wind; March of many weathers was being kind. This suited Jayne and Arthur well. They strolled in St Stephen's Green and had many long conversations, filling in the gaps in both their lives.

'It amazes me, Jayne, how forgiving you are; leaving you when you were a child was such a cruel thing to do,' Arthur confided during one of their walks. 'Of course I was young and selfish, and really believed I could have it all, Victoria, you, everything my way. I quickly learned this was not so; your mother actually did her best to keep me in your life, but your grandmother was having none of it, no forgiveness. It was hard to blame her, given my dreadful behaviour, but I loved you, wanted you in my life. When your mother passed away, I was sure I could take you with me and rear you myself. This was not to be; one obstacle after another was put in my way. My heart was broken, but I couldn't fix it and then we lost contact all together; shocking.' He put his arm around Jayne's shoulders as they walked. They were silent for a few minutes, a comfortable silence.

Arthur continued his story. 'Having decided to leave home for Victoria, I was on a hike to nowhere. Well, two very good things happened, Jess and George, your twin brother and sister. I really would love you all to know each other. They are always asking about you. In fact they made many attempts to contact you. You may not feel the same way, and I would understand that too. We can take it slowly and let things evolve in their own time.' He gave her an affectionate squeeze and they walked on in contented silence.

Towards the end of the week, Marcus decided to go to the States, intending to return to Ireland shortly to set up an office in Crannagh. He would leave his company in Detroit in the competent hands of his second in command. Also, he wanted to visit Louisa and tell her about events in Ireland, and break the news that he would be staying in Crannagh for quite some time. This part of the trip he was dreading.

'She's bound to cause an awful fuss, but it was her choice not to forgive and forget. She could have been part of all this. She could have had her family,' he said to Jayne just before he left.

She thought about his parting words long and hard. Later that evening, while alone with her father, she told him she would love to meet her brother and sister. As soon as she said it, a great peace came over her. Now, instead of being alone, she had her family; her baby would be surrounded by love, everything she had dreamed of.

Early in July, on a bright summer morning, baby James Arthur Jordan was born.

PART 3

Eighteen months later

Chapter 19

Magdalena stood looking out the window in the living room of her new house. Only recently completed, she still thought she was an intruder in somebody else's home. The end result was very pleasing and lived up to her dreams. Situated on an elevated piece of land, behind the old house, it commanded a striking view of the surrounding countryside: the mountains, forests, and pastures, with a distant view of the ocean. She decided on a Scandinavian style, and Marcus, together with his European colleague, met her demands and wishes. The interior boasted the sophisticated, clean lines of Northern European interior design.

From where she stood, Magdalena could look down on the big house. She still marvelled at the extraordinary restoration job with its exterior features restored to their former glory. The Folly stood in proud magnificence, surrounded by beautifully landscaped gardens. She was so deep in thought, she didn't hear the door open and Arthur Jordan coming in. He closed the door gently and made his way to her side, startling her when he put his hand on her shoulder.

'Happy?' he enquired.

'So happy. I cannot believe how beautiful it all is. Not just this house, but the whole place, The Folly, the stable yard, the cottages, the landscaped gardens, the walled garden, the orchard. It's amazing how it has come together after all the hard work.' Magdalena's enthusiasm was infectious.

'I have to agree with you, it has turned out as well and better than we ever imagined. We make a good team.' Arthur was talking about himself and Magdalena, Marcus and his team of architects and Jayne, who worked hard keeping little James, Lizzy and Edie contented and out of harm's way during the building work. James was now 18 months old and, like all children of that age, an absolute handful.

'Have you decided what you're doing yet?' Magdalena asked Arthur, in a light-hearted tone, much more light-hearted than she felt. They became very close during the past two years and their friendship was strengthening with each week that passed. She knew if he decided to leave, now that the work was done, she would miss him dreadfully. Arthur seemed unaware of Magdalena's growing affection for him.

'Typical man!' she thought to herself, 'Head in the clouds, happy to muddle along in our present, uncomplicated, relationship.'

They shared many enjoyable evenings together, either in the simple surroundings of The Village Hotel dining room, or bar, or in the slightly less salubrious surroundings of Mackey's Bar. On trips to Dublin, business or otherwise, they enjoyed revisiting the Shelbourne Hotel. On two occasions, Magdalena invited Arthur to join her on a trip abroad, to inspect several of her boutique hotels around the world. She always introduced him as her business associate. In truth, Arthur had no financial share in the newly founded business. He had stayed in Wicklow lending his engineering expertise to the project during its development.

Arthur had been more than happy to spend those months, now running into years, in Crannagh. He loved the place and more than anything else he wanted to spend as much time as possible with Jayne and his grandson. Having lost her for such a long time he now craved time together. His other children, George and Jessie, visited several times and already began to build a great friendship with Jayne.

'Isn't it just weird to think we've all been living on this planet for years and never knew each other,' Jessie exclaimed on more than one occasion during their visits. 'It's fabulous having a "big" sister.'

Jessie was infectiously good humoured and trusting and she embraced her new extended family with a big and open heart.

George, though willing to give it all a chance, was a bit more reticent and found it challenging that his father was so wrapped up in Jayne and James, he was more inclined to keep his feelings to himself.

Jayne, on the other hand, was overcome by the love and generosity afforded by her new family and loved them all. James, now a member of a large and caring family, along with Magdalena, Marcus, the Finn ladies, and Sarah, was a privileged young boy.

Arthur was not one to be tied down and so he told Magdalena that he would have to think a lot more about what he was going to do. She was a lady used to getting what she wanted and so urged him to stay on in Ireland. 'You are so welcome to come and share this house with me,' she told him. 'It is more than big enough for the two of us and of course, no strings attached.'

Arthur gave her a peck on the cheek and said gently: 'Let's wait and see.'

Chapter 20

When PR executive Sandra O'Leary left London on that drab morning in late January she was not sure she was making a good decision. Christmas away from home always left her with an aching desire to return to Ireland but this was the first time in the 12 years she had been in England that she gave in to homesickness. She had made a good life for herself, lived in a fashionable apartment, had a long term boyfriend and a very interesting job. Her social life was varied and at times full of fun. But something was missing and when she saw the advertisement in *The Times*, she thought about it a lot more than she usually would and try as she would she couldn't get it out of her head.

MANAGER REQUIRED FOR BOUTIQUE HOTEL IN CO. WICKLOW. 'FINN'S FOLLY' RESIDENTIAL AND HOLIDAY HOTEL, FOR ACTIVE, RETIRED LADIES AND GENTLEMEN, REQUIRES MANAGER/ ADMINISTRATOR. PLEASE APPLY TO MR MARCUS FENTON, FINN'S FOLLY HOTEL, CRANNAGH, CO. WICKLOW, IRELAND.

And so after several interviews and meetings with Edie, Lizzy, Magdalena, Jayne and Arthur, Sandra joined the team. They agreed unanimously on the name: Finn's Folly.

'Lizzy coined that name long ago when she heard about father's affair. She called the house Finn's Folly because she reckoned Nathaniel made a big mistake and we suffered by nearly losing the house,' Edie explained.

They all liked the name, feeling it lent a certain poignancy to the place, a little reminder of how it all came about that such a motley crew were now close friends, and also business associates. Sandra settled into

Crannagh, and within a short time she was an important part of the crew. She was a pretty girl, 32 years old and now single, as her boyfriend wouldn't consider the idea of moving to 'the backend of nowhere, in Ireland, of all places'.

Sandra's first job was to employ staff: chefs, kitchen staff, housekeepers, maids, waitresses, gardeners, chauffeurs and office staff. The interviews ran for weeks, with all the directors involved. Edie and Lizzy took a back seat, as they found the whole process tiring and tiresome. 'What are all these people going to do?' Lizzy asked in bewilderment. Life in The Folly, as she had always known it, was quiet and simple. 'All this fuss about nothing.' But in her heart she enjoyed all the excitement. Jayne was called in to give her opinion on several of the appointments, especially those involved with running the houses. To her delight, James was allotted a part-time nanny so she had plenty of time to spend with the ladies and to oversee the running of the household.

The dark, dreary days of January and February passed in a flurry of activity and then it was mid-March. The plan was to open in early summer and the next important move was to advertise the hotel and attract guests.

The village was buzzing with curiosity about all the goings-on in The Folly and Stasia was having a field day. She was privy to all sorts of information as lots of mail passed through her hands at the Post office and many of the new employees at Finn's Folly were unaware of her nosey temperament and chatted freely to her.

'Can you believe,' she whispered to one of her regulars, 'that Mia Finnegan from Wicklow town has applied for the job of housekeeper above at The Folly. She's nothing but an upstart. Never cleaned a house in her life. Notions she has; full of notions.'

Stasia was disgusted when Mia got the job and received great praise from Edie and Lizzy for the fine work she was doing.

The chef was selected from a large number of applicants. Ricardo was the favourite, as having run his own restaurant locally for years, they all knew him. He was Italian, married to an Irish girl, and his reputation for drama and hysterical outbursts, common to his Latino heritage, preceded him. He also had the reputation of being a magnificent chef. Ricardo was a character and would no doubt add great colour and panache to the establishment.

Lots of local boys and girls from the village were employed and everyone was delighted to see new jobs in the area. There was a staff house behind the stable yard for those who had too far to travel while on duty or for those working late shifts. Sandra O'Leary had a permanent apartment in the house and made a very comfortable home for herself. Jayne was delighted to have company of her own age living nearby and they became good friends. The nanny, Aine Sharkey, who doubled up as a carer for the Finn ladies, also lived at The Folly and although a little more shy and aloof than Sandra, little by little settled in and formed a firm friendship with the girls.

Sandra and Aine were naturally curious about Jayne and Marcus. They were such good friends, Marcus always at hand to advise and help Jayne in any way he could. He treated James with such love and affection he might have been his own child.

'Do you think they're a real item?' Aine asked Sandra during a coffee break one morning.

'It's hard to say,' replied Sandra, who didn't want to be gossipy yet couldn't help being curious. 'I suppose it's none of our business, but sure we'll eventually find out.'

They were more confused, when Marcus announced, that now the ground work was done, he would leave the choice of residents to Magdalena, Sandra, Edie and even Lizzy, if she was interested. He also suggested to Magdalena and Edie that Jayne should be involved, as 'she has a wise head on her shoulders'. He was going back to the States indefinitely, but would of course be in constant close contact.

'He's obviously not too interested in settling down here, if he's off to the States,' Aine remarked.

Sandra had to agree with her. 'It's a pity he's going,' she said. 'He is a breath of fresh air around the place.

Chapter 21

No one was more surprised than Jayne when Marcus announced his departure. She had grown so fond of him and James was devoted to him, she couldn't imagine life without him. She was puzzled and upset but couldn't bring herself to ask him why he was going. She presumed her feelings for him were not matched by his for her. Over the previous two years they spent a lot of time together but in retrospect, their relationship did not develop but rather had settled into a comfortable friendship. Maybe that was all Marcus expected or wanted. Jayne had grown in self-confidence since Arthur's return and James's birth but she was still slow to express her feelings and so accepted the situation without question. There were a lot of important matters to be sorted out, not least marketing and advertising the hotel, so putting Marcus out of her head, as best she could, she decided to get on with the job.

Marcus sat at the bar of Mackey's pub, nursing a pint of beer. It was early evening and the bar was quiet. He was lost in his thoughts wondering where it had all gone wrong. All that time ago after the tragedy of the fire he had been so sure Jayne and he had a future together. Now, almost two years later, here he was, estranged from the one person he truly loved. And now, to add to the emotional turmoil, he loved little James also. What a mess! He thought they had become really close but every time he tried to confide his true feelings to Jayne, it didn't work out. He was a loser, an emotional coward, and now he was leaving Crannagh, and finally putting a nail in his own coffin. He missed every chance he was given and hadn't a clue how to make it better. He was certain Jayne just didn't feel for him what he felt for her.

Another week and he'd be back in the States and it would all be over.

'Hi stranger! Not talking to anyone tonight?' Marcus was jolted from his day dreaming and swung around on his stool. He was much relieved to see it was Sarah standing beside him, he had always liked her. He found her sincere and direct, she called a spade a spade and yet had a heart of gold.

'Sarah!' Marcus exclaimed, 'What are you doing here?'

'Oh, glad to see you too Marcus,' Sarah replied good humouredly. 'I have a few unexpected days off and thought I'd come to stay with my favourite people. I haven't even told Jayne I'm coming, so I hope it suits.'

'You visiting always suits,' Marcus assured her.

'I just dropped off to use the bathroom and freshen up, before heading out to The Folly. I spotted you and thought: "There's a nice man who'll buy me a drink".' She sat up on the stool next to Marcus, and they chatted together.

An hour later Sarah emerged from the pub puzzled and bewildered. During their long chat Marcus had confided to her all his mixed emotions about himself and Jayne and his great disappointment their relationship never went beyond friendship. Sarah questioned his judgement, asking was he sure about what he was saying. For the first time since she had known him, Marcus became irritated with her, so she backed off, realising he was a very upset man. He apologised for being rude, but she could see he was emotional and she listened, rather than spoke. When they parted company, Sarah said she was going out to the cottage and hoped she'd see him later. It looked to her as though he planned to find comfort in a glass rather than anywhere else.

Driving out to The Folly Sarah decided it was time for action, time for her to prove her true friendship with Jayne and to play cupid. What was the best thing to do? She knew Marcus had it all wrong, that Jayne loved him and she knew it would break their hearts if someone didn't bang their heads together and make them see sense. That someone had to be her. She decided to act promptly as Marcus was not planning to hang around Crannagh much longer.

She phoned Arthur: 'Where are you?' Her abruptness surprised him but he sensed it was important. 'Can you babysit James for a little while, please. I need to take Jayne out?' Arthur said he'd be there in ten minutes.

Half an hour later, Sarah and Jayne arrived at Mackey's pub, Sarah's fingers crossed that Marcus would still be there. She needn't have worried. He was sitting exactly as she had left him, still gazing into a rather flat looking pint of beer. Taking Jayne by the arm, she steered her through the now crowded room to the counter. Her heart was racing and she could feel herself breaking out in a cold sweat. Reaching Marcus's side, she pulled a stool alongside him and almost pushed Jayne onto it.

'Now,' she declared, 'this might be the last time either of you talk to me, so let me explain that the reason I'm here is because you are my two dearest friends, I love you both, and I know something that you should know.' Marcus and Jayne looked alarmed. Before either of them could speak, Sarah, caught them both and gently pressed their heads together.

'I know, that you love each other and I also know you don't know how to say it, so now I've done my bit. Goodbye!' She turned on her heels, and without looking back, ran from the pub.

Arriving back at the cottage, Sarah found Arthur sitting on the floor playing cars with James. It was past his bed time but Arthur paid little heed to the rules and regulations regarding his grandson's routine. They were happy and at first didn't notice Sarah. Arthur eventually lifting his head was surprised to see her.

'You're back early. Not much of a night out.'

'I have a bit of a headache. Jayne stayed with a few friends at the pub.'

Sarah didn't feel she was really lying, because with all the carry on that evening, following a long day at work, she was wrecked and certainly had a nagging headache.

'I'll look after James till Jayne gets back, if you like.'

Arthur was happy enough to leave them at it and head out for the evening himself. Before he left, he asked Sarah if she thought Jayne was a bit out of sorts.

'She seems preoccupied and down in herself. It's probably nothing.'

Sarah agreed, saying she might have needed a night out and a bit of fun, time away from minding the Finns and the baby.

'So true,' Arthur remarked and headed off.

When Sarah had put James to bed, she collapsed onto the sofa with a mug of tea, contemplating the events of the night and what she had done. She became more and more nervous as time went by, wondering if it was a good or a bad sign that Jayne had not returned yet. After another hour, she panicked, and phoned Sandra O'Leary.

'Are you at home, Sandra?' she asked, trying without success to sound calm. Sandra heard the tone in her voice and without hesitation said she was on her way over to the cottage.

'So what you're telling me is, you told Jayne and Marcus they love each other and they need to get their act together and you haven't heard from either of them since?'

Sandra had opened a bottle of wine and the two girls were sitting comfortably in front of the fire.

'Yeah! That's more or less it in a nutshell,' Sarah replied. She was much more relaxed and stopped believing she had caused a major catastrophe.

'Sounds fair enough to me. I believe you're right and even if you're not, other than a bit of embarrassment all round, no harm done.'

Before long all was revealed. The cottage door burst open and Jayne stood there, a look of anger on her face.

'Well Sarah, I hope you're proud of yourself! I have never in my whole life felt like this!' Sarah was horrified until Jayne's face broke into a broad smile, her eyes lighting up.

'I repeat,' she said, 'I have never felt like this in my whole life! I have never been so happy!' At that moment, on cue, Marcus came through the door and they put their arms around one another.

Chapter 22

When they had set up an interview panel for prospective residents of Finn's Folly, Sandra made a proposal to Magdalena, Edie, Lizzy and Marcus: 'I suggest we play it safe and do it so that you people have a choice of residents but they think they are coming here to approve the place. It will work both ways. Also at this point I would like to wish Jayne and Marcus a life of happiness together. We are all so pleased to hear of their engagement.'

Everyone in the room gave a cheer and a round of applause. They were all delighted Marcus had changed his mind about returning to the States and about the forthcoming nuptials.

'Now, back to business!' Sandra continued when the room settled down again. 'Firstly I would like to suggest that Jayne and Arthur be involved in the selection process. Obviously, you have all worked closely as a team to bring the project this far and I suspect you would like to keep your team intact.' This suggestion was met with full approval from everyone and the plan was set in motion.

On two weekends in April, Finn's Folly would throw a welcome day reception, an afternoon cocktail party, catered for by Ricardo the chef and his team. The guests on each occasion would be carefully selected from the applicants, of whom there were many, requests for residential places having flowed in following the advertising campaign. 'The Folly Gang', as they now called themselves, would entertain and mingle with the guests and after the party, meet again to make their choices. Everyone would have different opinions but at least they hoped to reject anyone who was really not suitable.

'A good eclectic mix of people is what we should aim for!' Magdalena said. 'Hopefully this place will offer more than just somewhere to live so we all benefit from each other and have fun!'

'Hear! Hear!' Arthur agreed as did the others.

The plan was made, now the work had to begin. The intervening weeks passed in a haze of frenetic activity. Everyone put their best foot forward. Even Lizzy, proud as punch to be hosting such wonderful house parties, 'just like the old days', was cheerful and interested, not nearly so critical as usual. The ladies donned their finery and set out to enjoy themselves.

Both parties were a success. On day one, following the early and dramatic arrival of Dame Beatrice McCourt, all else paled into insignificance. She was an archetypal eccentric bringing with her all the arrogant charm and colour of your most fanciful peacock.

'Darlings!' she proclaimed as she made her entrance. 'What a dear little house!'

There was a momentary stunned silence, until Marcus saved the day.

'My dear Dame Beatrice, how lovely to see you.' He made all the introductions and before Lizzy could confront her about her 'little house' remark, he guided her through the drawing room and through the open French doors into the garden.

It was a beautiful day, unseasonably warm for early April. The newly planted spring bulbs were in full bloom, enhancing the charm of the landscaped gardens. All the old foliage and ancient trees had been preserved and gave the gardens an air of timelessness, casting their shadows on the well-manicured lawns. As the rest of the guests arrived the drama of Dame Beatrice's entrance was forgotten, for now.

Professor Isaac Thorn and his wife Matilda were great favourites but they admitted they 'were perhaps a little bit ambitious in their desire to reside at Finn's Folly' as they were 'not very wealthy'. Sandra assured them that they had many options on accommodation, with variables rates. They were visibly delighted as they had fallen in love with the place. Ricardo and his staff produced a magnificent feast of party food, mouth-watering canapés that would please any palate while wine and cocktails flowed freely.

'The food is divine!' Peter Daly declared as he and his partner Tony Purcell tucked into the delicious fare. Turning to Edie and Magdalena, he added: 'Let me tell you if this is anything to go by, me and my Tony will be here in the morning.' It transpired these two gentlemen friends (as Lizzy liked to refer to them), had recently retired from running a very successful city restaurant and sold their business at a healthy profit.

'The stories we could tell you, my dears, would have your hair standing on end. Thirty years wining and dining the rich and famous, an endless series of intrigue and romance. You'd love it.'

Magdalena certainly had these two on her list of probables. She could foresee lots of fun and entertainment in their company.

Dame Beatrice, now well fuelled with gin and wine, wandered over to Tony and Peter. 'Tell me,' she said, 'are you gay?'

Without drawing breath, Peter replied: 'Of course my dear! And you tell me, are you really as pretentious and obnoxious as you appear?'

'So I'm told. But I have my good points too. I like cats.'

Magdalena and Edie, who were joined by several of the others, looked on in amazement. They realised drama and entertainment would not be in short supply if this lot came to stay. Another favourite was the Major.

'Every establishment such as Finn's Folly, must have "A Major",' Marcus declared.

He was arrogant and loud with a booming, resonant voice that commanded the attention of anyone in the vicinity. Dame Beatrice, on first hearing him, exclaimed in her own inimitable manner: 'Who is that ghastly little man?'

Sandra couldn't help sniggering but pulling herself together replied: 'That, Dame Beatrice, is Major Geoffrey Thompson; let me introduce you.'

'My dear lady, how charming,' the Major gushed when Sandra introduced him, sweeping a slight bow as he took her outstretched hand and kissed it. Thankfully, Dame Beatrice was enchanted with his 'wonderful manners' and they proceeded to have a long and animated conversation.

'Phew, that went better than expected,' Sandra sighed and left them to it.

And so the day progressed and as evening fell and the party drew to a close The Folly Gang were left with plenty to think about.

Chapter 23

Eve Langton was in her sitting room, sipping a cup of coffee and looking out on her garden, deep in thought. She had been in Ireland for fourteen months and was disappointed she had not settled into her new home very well. She was lonely. She couldn't say she was homesick, as she had no home to miss but she was sad she had to leave her native Texas to start a new life. At 66 it seemed like a fairly drastic decision, but she had no choice. When her 41 year marriage ended, following the arrest and conviction of her husband for murder, she knew she had to leave. Fortunately, and there were very few reasons at that time to count her blessings, she had a very successful and lucrative career. As a scientist and designer, working in a multi-national home hygiene production company, she was directly involved, in the invention and marketing of a massively successful new product, which had gone global. When her husband's ill-gotten gains were seized as criminal assets, her personal fortune was left intact.

It had taken her a long time to come to terms with those terrible events. She found it difficult to believe she had lived a lie with a man who was now a stranger to her. She felt deceived and cheated but most of all, stupid. How had she never noticed what was going on, right under her nose, often in her own home? Her husband was a cheat and a fraud, leaving unsuspecting people bereft of their savings, the final horror when he was eventually found out, being the murder of a policeman. Now on death row in Texas, he was the part of her life she had to leave behind. To get as far away as possible, mentally and geographically, she decided to come to Ireland. She had no living connections there, but often listened to her grandparents wax lyrical about the beauty and culture of their native country. They left when they were young and had never returned.

Eve decamped to Bettystown, a small seaside village on the east coast north of Dublin that was busy in the summer but quiet in the winter months, just what she wanted. But it proved too solitary for Eve. She lived a sociable life in the States and the contrast in Ireland was too sharp. While in this sad frame of mind Eve first spotted the advertisement for Finn's Folly. There and then she decided to apply.

On the same day that Eve Langton's application arrived on Sandra O'Leary's desk, so also did one from Colin and Margaret Smyth who, like Eve Langton, had been married for over 40 years. They raised a family of four sons, all of whom emigrated to far flung places after finishing their education. Margaret was inclined to see their leaving as a criticism of her capacity to make a happy home. Colin reassured her that this was not the case, as most young men flew the nest at a certain stage of their lives, especially growing up in a dull, middle-class suburb of a city like Dublin. Dublin in the '80s was an unexciting, drab place, compared to alternative cities full of excitement and opportunity. Now, quite unexpectedly, their eldest son had decided to return to live in Ireland with his wife and family.

On hearing the news, Margaret confided her concern to Colin: 'It will be a huge adjustment for them all, after living in Australia for so long.'

'Now woman,' he replied gently, 'you relax, they're well able to make up their own minds. You just be happy.'

Within a couple of weeks and after lots of negotiations, Colin and Margaret's son agreed to buy the family home in Stillorgan, leaving his parents free to make new plans for their retirement years. It appeared everyone was happy and the plan to move to Finn's Folly was a great source of pleasure to the couple.

'We could have a right good time, little to do except please ourselves,' Colin declared enthusiastically.

Enda Maher

Around the same time as the Smyths applied to Finn's Folly, a letter arrived at the house enquiring about a long-stay arrangement. It was from Mary Forde, presently living in Dublin. She was a different kettle of fish, a dark horse who rarely socialised, single in the true sense of the word with little interest in other people. She had one sister with whom she kept up sporadic contact. She invested her inheritance from her parents wisely and now in her 60th year was a woman of considerable means. All her life she had suffered from obsessive compulsive disorder, OCD, and never being properly treated, she was an anxious, eccentric soul. She managed it well, provided she had no interference from outsiders but recently she began to suffer from isolation and loneliness; hence her interest in Finn's Folly.

Chapter 24

On a chilly, windswept day in April, Mary Forde caught the train from Dublin to Wicklow where Harry O'Riordan, the chauffeur from Finn's Folly was due to collect her. Unknown to her, he was also collecting several others including Colin and Margaret Smyth and Eve Langton coming from Bettystown. It was the day of the second welcoming party. Unlike the first one, the day was dark and miserable, it was raining heavily with clouds low on the hills like a shroud.

The staff at the house started work early to put in an extra effort, to capture the atmosphere, as Mother Nature was certainly not on side that day. The view from the windows was non-existent, the gardens, hills and sky obliterated by thick cloud yielding heavy rain and a dense, damp mist. The gloom was more than adequately counterbalanced by the brightly lit rooms, with their subtle mood lighting, the open fires and gentle background music. Ricardo, who was proving to be a firm favourite was creating all sorts of culinary delights to woo their guests. Overall, first impressions were certainly going to be very good.

When the party finished that evening, Magdalena was very tired. She had put all her energy into it, and now that she was home again, she wanted to kick off her shoes and put her feet up. There was a meeting the following day, in the main house, to select the residents. She wished that Arthur was there to support her, but he left for Scotland during the week, and didn't say when he would return. Not alone was she very fond of him, she also trusted his judgement, especially when it came to people. She thought she was a fairly good judge of character, after all her years in business, but was sometimes misguided by her frivolous female side. Such was the case now. She liked the Professor and his wife, Matilda, and never doubted they would make wonderful guests but much to Arthur's dismay, she also loved Dame Beatrice's flamboyance and questionable charm. She had done her best to engage the Dame in serious conversation, trying to find out who she really was. By the end of a lengthy conversation she learned little, although Beatrice talked incessantly about herself. Magdalena wondered would any of the others support her in recommending Beatrice as a future resident of Finn's Folly. Thinking about the other candidates, Eve Langton seemed a sincere, likeable woman but she struck Magdalena as mysterious, as if she was hiding something.

As she was mulling this over, there was a knock on the hall door. Magdalena had let Sinead, her maid, go home early following the party so she dragged herself up from the comfort of her couch, muttering, to answer the door. It was Sandra O'Leary whom she'd seen at the main house less than an hour ago.

'Sandra!' Magdalena exclaimed, 'Is everything alright?'

'Yes, yes, of course,' replied Sandra, a little flustered. 'I'm sorry to disturb you, you must be very tired after the party. It was a great success, wasn't it?'

Magdalena was well aware Sandra was not there to discuss the day's events, so inviting her into the sitting room, she asked Sandra why she called.

'Just after you all left the house, who should arrive out of the blue, only Dame Beatrice McCourt. She was looking for you Magdalena,' Sandra paused, monitoring Magdalena's reaction. 'Perhaps I should have told her it was too late to visit but she was very persistent and surprisingly humble. She almost seemed distressed. Anyway I left her in my office and said I'd see if you were available.' She paused, looking uncomfortable. 'I hope I did the right thing. I just sensed I shouldn't turn her away.'

'You were absolutely right,' said Magdalena. 'It's important to go with your gut feeling. Why don't you fetch her, while I tidy myself and put on my shoes.'

She smiled reassuringly at Sandra and continued: 'By the way, thanks for coming over yourself, rather than putting me on the spot on the phone.'

Arriving at the house, Dame Beatrice returned Magdalena's warm greeting and apologised for her unexpected visit. Magdalena thought she looked rather pale, tired and a little sad as Sandra had said.

'It is a pleasure to see you, Beatrice,' Magdalena assured her, offering her a glass of wine.

Settling themselves into the sofa in the study, Magdalena chatted away, leaving it up to her visitor to say why she had called. Sipping her wine and joining in the small talk, Beatrice finally got to the point.

'I'm sure you're wondering what brought me here tonight. When I met you at the welcoming party last week I thought you were a person I could trust and relate to. I hope I'm not being presumptuous.'

Magdalena listened carefully without interrupting. She had dealt with enough awkward situations in her life to realise this conversation was not easy for Beatrice.

'What I want to do, is tell you how hugely important it is for me to acquire a place in Finn's Folly. I know people think I'm a bit spoilt and arrogant and leaving the party, I knew I had not endeared myself to anyone, especially the Finn ladies, Jayne or Marcus. For me that day, was revealing and humbling. Everyone was kind and generous and welcoming and I fear I behaved in my usual selfish, self-centred manner. It's been a very long time since I enjoyed the company of real people, sincere people and I want to ask your forgiveness for my behaviour in the hope you'll reconsider me as a resident.' She paused, a slight flush on her cheeks and the very smallest hint of tears brimming in her eyes.

Magdalena felt sympathy for this woman, this relative stranger.

'We have not made a final decision on the residents as yet,' she explained. 'In fact we have a meeting about it in the morning. Before that we can make no decisions, but of course we will seriously consider your application, Beatrice.'

Her visitor looked relieved and more relaxed.

'You may wonder about my title, and my wealth. Well both are genuine but certainly new in a very humble life. May I briefly tell you my story, Magdalena?'

Chapter 25

Having topped up their wine, the two women settled down for what was a very interesting story. Beatrice was born to poor parents in post-war Russia. The family lived in a small village and the children grew up during the grim years of the Cold War. Times were hard, but, from an early age the young Beatrice showed enormous talent as a ballerina. She was nurtured by the Soviet government and when she was 9 sent to study in Moscow. At first homesick and lonely for her family as time went by she became completely wrapped up in her training. As a young woman in the '60s and '70s, Beatrice toured Europe with the Russian State Ballet, until aged 20, she defected to the USA. From there she made her way to Europe, earning a reputation for excellence.

'I was the archetypal primadonna and that has stayed with me all my life. I moved to the UK and 10 years ago was made a Dame. It was a great honour, but now that I am older, alone and lonely, it all means very little to me. I crave a happy, uncomplicated life for my latter years and I want to spend it here. I fell in love with this beautiful place and all the people I met. I will be a much better resident than first impressions suggested ... I promise!'

Her almost childlike expression brought a smile to Magdalena's face. She could see that this hard, toffee-nosed primadonna had a whole different side to her, one she liked.

When Dame Beatrice left, Magdalena decided to share her story with Marcus and Jayne. It was getting late but she strolled down to the stable yard and was pleased to find them at home and still up. They found the Dame saga fascinating and were definitely swayed in her favour for approval at the next day's meeting.

'I was thinking of offering her the apartment in my house,' Magdalena said. 'I'd like the company, I think we'd get on. In fact, I'd say we have a lot in common.'

She sat on for a while, comfortable in the surroundings of the well extended but still very cosy cottage.

'Well,' she said, 'I'm going to be nosey. Any plans for the wedding?'

'Lots of plans, all being kept under wraps until The Folly is up and running. That won't be long now.'

Jayne and Marcus had in fact talked a great deal about their future. They had many options, including a life in the United States, which initially sounded attractive but was not what either of them wanted. Marcus remained chief executive of the architectural company but with a competent deputy in charge he was happy to stay in Ireland and visit the States on a fairly regular basis to check the business.

One evening as they strolled in the woods with James he confided to Jayne: 'It's weird but I feel that Ireland is my home and America is a foreign place now. I never set foot in Ireland until my visit with Louisa. Sorry to mention the war,' he added, smiling at the thought of his errant mother. Jayne returned his amused expression and squeezing his arm declared that she too would much prefer to stay in Ireland and raise James in his native country.

'I'd feel wrong separating him from all his family and friends here, even though he has the best Dad in the world. I hated not knowing my family.'

'That's settled so, we'll stay here in Wicklow and work away at running the hotel. We can always go to visit your brother and sister in Canada and your Dad in Scotland and of course, Abigail in South Africa. We'll do lots of travelling. OK? You happy with that?' Jayne was more than happy.

Speaking to Sarah later she said: 'Can you believe that I am now surrounded by family and really good friends. What a lucky break I got when I moved to Crannagh. It's all thanks to you Sarah.' Sarah responded in her usual glib fashion: 'Sure I know I'm wonderful! Now what about the wedding?'

'Will you come down for a few days to help plan it. You know men, Marcus's attention span for wedding discussions is rather limited. Let's Sandra, you and me, get our heads together on it and we'll pass it all with Marcus. He'll be delighted to be let off the hook.'

'Brilliant, I'll be there. You name the day.'

'First we've got a hotel to open. We're almost there. Just a few more weeks and everyone will have settled in, I hope.'

Chapter 26

By the third week in May, the hotel was ready for the residents to move in. It was a lovely early summer that year, lots of bright sunshine and little cloud or rain. The early flowering shrubs and the masses of rhododendrons were in full bloom, emblazoning The Folly garden with colour. The selection meeting had gone smoothly and despite some grumbling from Lizzy about those 'gay' men, and her reservations about Beatrice, they managed to agree on their choice of residents.

Jayne approached Magdalena and Sandra O'Leary with an idea she had been mulling over for some time.

'What would you think about Edie and Lizzy moving back into the main house. I know they love their cottage, but it was really forced upon them by the fire. They grew up in The Folly, and now that it's so well restored and so "posh", I feel they might like to move back. Should we give them the option anyway?'

'And what about their cottage? Any ideas for that?'

Jayne had thought that one out and explained that she reckoned Tony and Peter would love to live in the stable yard. 'After all,' she continued, 'they were chefs in their former life, and once a chef, always a chef. In the cottage they could cook or not. Edie and Lizzy rarely cook for themselves now. They probably wouldn't miss the kitchen one bit.'

The ladies were enthralled with the idea of moving back into the house and started to plan it straight away. They had also decided that to keep the house alive with memories of bygone days, they would name the suites after family members, past and present. And so, having vacated their cottage with twinges of regret, Edie and Lizzy moved back into Finn's Folly Hotel, to The Olivia Suite, overlooking the garden and looking directly down on the little woodland where Dorothea's ashes were spread.

'I like feeling so close to her,' Lizzy remarked to Eddie on their first evening, as they prepared to go to the cocktail bar for pre-dinner drinks.

In the suite next to the Finn ladies, Eve Langton was settling in to her new home, with an excitement she had not felt for a long time. She was very comfortable with this move, convinced it would solve her loneliness problems. She did wonder wryly what her fellow guests would think if they knew she was the wife of a murderer on death row. 'Does anyone ever really know what goes on in other people's lives,' she thought to herself as she left her rooms, The Astrid Suite, to go for a drink in the bar. She also planned to ask those nice Finn ladies the origin of the different names. 'Astrid,' she thought, 'is a beautiful name. I wonder what story she would tell, were she here today.' She reminded herself, that she must take care not to let her guard down or reveal her secret.

The house came alive during that first day of moving. There was a buzz of conversation in the cocktail bar where Marcus decided to play host that night, along with the young barman from the village. The bar was closed to outsiders this first night, to allow people get to know each other.

Tony and Peter engaged Prof. Thorn and his wife Matilda in conversation about the merits or otherwise of microwave ovens. The Professor had a keen interest in food, having spent his career researching nutrients.

'My dears,' declared Tony, 'now that we are neighbours in the stable yard, perhaps you would honour us with your company for dinner one evening.'

Margaret and Colin Smyth sat quietly by the window, enjoying the view of the garden. Colin was really excited when they received their notice of acceptance from Finn's Folly; Margaret was not quite so enthralled. She was a quiet, self-contained woman who liked to read and walk and go to the theatre now and again. She was not an extrovert like her husband and hoped she would be content living among a lot of other people. However she was prepared to give it a go and she loved the energy Colin put into everything they did. For him, this move to The Folly was a big adventure, for Margaret it had been a bit of a trauma. Her spirits had certainly risen when they were shown to their new quarters, The Louisa Suite.

Little did she or any of the other guests know, the trouble caused, when Jayne suggested calling one suite after Marcus's mother.

'Well,' she explained, 'she is his mother, I'm going to be Marcus's wife, which makes her my mother-in-law, and James will be her grandson. We can't pretend she doesn't exist.'

Lizzy sniffed, and fumbled with her handkerchief. She was disgusted with the idea of involving Louisa in any way in the hotel; she never forgave her, one tiny bit, for what she did to the family. Anyway, Edie and the others agreed with Jayne, and so The Louisa Suite it was.

On her arrival earlier that day Magdalena suggested to Beatrice for her first night they should dine together. The apartment was a big hit with the Dame and she was more than happy with her spacious living room, large dining room and kitchen, (which she had no intention of using), and her bedrooms with beautiful bathrooms attached. There was a connecting door to Magdalena's house, but this could be locked and the bright red front door opened onto the garden and terrace, sloping down the hill towards the orchard and the main house. Sinead O'Hehir, Kathleen's niece, worked as Magdalena's maid and was willing to look after Dame Beatrice also. Magdalena was a kind and fair employer and Sinead hoped her other employer would be the same. When she mentioned this to Jayne and Aine Sharkey, they both laughed: 'I wouldn't bet on it.' Beatrice had a lot of work to change the first impression she made at the selection party.

Magdalena and Beatrice cut quite a dash gliding into the dining room in their finery. While Beatrice seated herself at their table, Magdalena circulated around the room welcoming the new arrivals. Tony greeted her effusively, jumping up, and kissing her on both cheeks.

'I'm astonished to see that ghastly Dame whatever her name is. I never expected she'd be considered after her shocking carry-on at the party.'

Peter kicked him under the table as Magdalena remarked: 'One should never judge the book by the cover.' She hoped Beatrice didn't hear Tony's loud whisper above the hum of conversation in the room and made up her mind to try to sort out that relationship, if she could, sooner rather than later.

Everyone settled down to enjoy a delicious meal prepared by Ricardo. The two local teenagers from the village who waited on tables, were well trained by Sandra O'Leary. They were friendly and helpful and waited until they were safely out of earshot in the kitchen, before they giggled about the rather strange people they were serving. There was no doubt they were a motley crew. A little later the Major arrived, adding to the atmosphere of the evening. Robust and ebullient as ever, he burst into the room, greeting everyone like long lost friends. He was nothing if not cheerful, declaring to Magdalena he 'found The Nathaniel Suite, absolutely charming'. Margaret Smyth made a mental note to give him the slip, if she saw him approaching.

Chapter 27

Mary Forde did not make an appearance at dinner that night, in fact she didn't arrive until the next day. On the day she received her letter of acceptance from Finn's Folly she was battling with one of her more common demons: her pet anxiety of colour co-ordinating everything in her house. She could usually limit the frenetic tidying of her presses and wardrobe to one room, but today, possibly because of the stress related to a move, by 10.30 in the morning she had already gone through her bedroom, bathroom and was now starting on the kitchen. Today's colours, which had to be stashed away out of sight, were orange and bright green. All offending articles of clothing, foot wear, hats, bags, towels had been piled up by the back door, ready for removal and storage in the attic of her detached garage. It was an exhausting and tedious job and already Mary felt tired. She sat down at the kitchen table and having read the letter, was overwhelmed with anxiety. A move to Finn's Folly suddenly seemed an insurmountable burden, one she couldn't possibly handle. She felt the panic coming on, and from years of the same unhappy experiences, she knew what to do. She ran to her bedroom, took a sleeping tablet, and hid under the duvet, abandoning all her belongings in the hall.

Lying in the security of the darkness, she thought about her next move. The phobic terrors of obsessive compulsive disorder, had dominated her life since her early teens, sometimes more so than others and she dearly wished to be rid of the horrible controlling condition. Where it began was hard to discern. She came from an average, middle-class family brought up in suburban Dublin during the '50s and '60s.

Perhaps, her counsellor thought, it was the Roman Catholic influences of those times that had damaged her sensitive mind. Ireland then was ridden with guilt and shame. Original sin, immodesty, impurity were the catch phrases in the convent school and often at home. Those times were a far cry from the present day when promiscuity and hedonism made life such fun and so stress free for young people growing up in Ireland. She fell asleep, and several hours later awoke, refreshed and less upset, the panic having abated. She knew what she was going to do. She would place her house and all her belongings, bar a few things to bring with her, in the hands of an auctioneer. She would ask her sister to help sort out her personal belongings and give them away appropriately, either to relatives or charity shops.

Having made the decision and followed through with her plan, armed with one suitcase, Mary Forde left her house for the last time to catch the train to Wicklow. She was due to arrive at Finn's Folly the day after the official moving date, as she could never make such a big change in her life on a Saturday. Shedding her baggage of many years, and with as few belongings as possible, she was determined to make a new start and do everything to subdue her anxieties and enjoy the rest of her life.

Meanwhile, with all the activity in The Folly, Magdalena missed several phone calls from Arthur. For over a week now, he argued with himself about staying in Scotland or moving back to Wicklow. He loved his independence, but also loved his new family life with Jayne and James and now, of course Marcus, his son-in-law to be. Magdalena also wangled her way into his affections and he had to admit he missed her company. He could as easily visit the twins in Canada from Ireland as Scotland, and they loved coming to Wicklow for holidays. The arguments in favour of Ireland were mounting up.

Katy, his young neighbour, dropped in and over a cup of coffee she more or less put her finger on the solution.

'Why not just go there, stay for as long as you want and keep your place here; come back in a while if you miss me too much!'

They laughed but Arthur knew she made a lot of sense: keep his options open.

On the third Sunday in May Mary Forde arrived in a taxi at Finn's Folly just as Arthur Jordan drew up in his car. Meeting in the doorway, they introduced themselves and made their way inside. Mary was delighted to meet such a charming person and felt her confidence growing as she announced her arrival to Sandra O'Leary.

'You are so welcome, Miss Forde. You should have let us know you were on the way and I'd have sent the car to the station to collect you.'

She took Mary's suitcase and placed it by the reception desk.

'Tell me, when can we expect delivery of your belongings?' She looked taken aback when Mary said her suitcase contained everything she needed.

'Very good,' she said quickly, hiding her surprise. 'Let me show you to your suite, it's The Elizabeth Suite and when you are ready, I will serve afternoon tea in the drawing room.'

Arthur failed to find Magdalena at home and made his way to the stable yard hoping to see Jayne or Marcus. Jayne was busy weeding while James played with his toys. Before she noticed her father standing watching them, he felt a surge of happiness at the sight of his daughter and grandson and knew he made the right decision to return to live in Wicklow. Jayne was thrilled to see him and James squealed with delight, toddling into his arms immediately.

'What are you doing here Dad?' Jayne enquired. 'I didn't expect to see you just yet.'

'I missed you all too much,' he replied, cuddling James as he spoke. 'I thought I'd take Magdalena up on her offer to stay at her house. What do you think?'

'I think you're too late Dad. Dame Beatrice has just moved in with her and they both seem very happy with the arrangement.'

Arthur put James down, very taken aback. 'That scandalous old bat!' he declared. 'I'm surprised she was even accepted, let alone got the pick of the bunch.'

Although Jayne laughed she could see Arthur was upset, 'Well,' she continued, 'you wouldn't make a commitment, and let me tell you, Magdalena's not one to hang around. She gets on with things. And by the way, the Dame is not nearly as obnoxious as we first thought.'

'We'll wait and see.' Arthur was not going to make any rash decisions about Beatrice. 'Now tell me all the news.'

Chapter 28

While Arthur and Jayne were catching up on recent events at the hotel, Stasia wasted no time spreading their news in the village. The comings and goings from Finn's Folly, were well noted, ready to be passed on to the first willing listener who came her way. The local girls and boys who worked part time at the hotel were more than happy to describe in detail the eccentricities of the new residents. Stasia encouraged them to call into the post office and give her a run down on the latest events.

'Did you hear?' she reported to her customers. 'There's a big wedding coming up at The Folly. That Marcus, from America, is making an honest woman of Jayne Jordan. I suppose it will be a good thing to give that child a father.'

'My God, Stasia, but you've got a wicked tongue,' replied one local woman. 'Can you never see the good in anything or anyone? I think it's wonderful to hear some happy news for a change. There's enough misery around. That terrible fire and poor Kathleen's and Astrid's deaths left them all floundering up there. I think they're amazing getting it all going again.'

Stasia was not to be put down and shook her head knowingly, adding: 'We'll see. It seems to me that place is attracting strange characters into the area.'

'For God's sake Stasia, it's a hotel for retired people, not young offenders and criminals. You make it sound like a probation facility.'

The customer left the post office, looking dismayed. Where did gossips like Stasia come from? Stasia was not discouraged and was determined to find out exactly what was what and who was who. She was in this state of watchful, high alert, when Jack Redmond came into the post office, asking for directions to The Folly.

'Finn's Folly, is it?' Stasia was now very excited, for some reason she felt this man was going to be newsworthy.

'And tell me,' she said, looking him up and down, 'what brings you this way? Holidays, is it?'

'Private family business,' he snapped back.

Stasia was not so easily deterred. 'So you're a relation of the Finns then, are you?' she persisted. She took in his appearance in some detail while interrogating him. He was a man around his mid-40s, tall, fairly slim and fit looking, with that swarthy skin that gives the appearance of an all year tan, dressed casually but expensively. He was staring at her now, irritated. She noticed his brown eyes had narrowed into an angry glare.

'Whether or not I'm a relation of anyone is absolutely none of your business, my good woman. Now will you give me directions, or should I go elsewhere?'

Realising she was getting nowhere with this rather arrogant man, Stasia told him what he wanted to know. Barely thanking her, he turned on his heels and left.

Jack had hardly been in touch with Jayne since the baby's birth. Saving his marriage and his job had been his priority. But Vanessa had left with the children and the dogs, telling Jack he was 'a lazy, philandering, good-for-nothing, boring asshole'. He needed to reinvent himself and his life. His banking job was not what it used to be, the recession had seen to that. Salary cuts and no chance of promotion left him floundering. He was insecure and insulted by his wife's remarks and departure. And so with his injured pride dragging him down, he intended to pick up where he had left off and get to know his son.

Arriving at the gates of Finn's Folly, Jack was taken aback at the magnificence of the old house and gardens, with the stunning backdrop of the mountains. Deciding to be discreet, he parked his car outside the gates and walked up the long avenue. This would give him time to plan a strategy. He supposed it was not all going to be simple, he couldn't just ask to see his son and take him off for the day. That was how he thought it should be. 'But then,' he thought, 'women can be awkward and prone to dramatics. Vanessa certainly was. Fancy calling him a good-for-nothing . . . and the rest.' By the time he got his head around these unsavoury thoughts he was half way up the avenue. Beatrice and Magdalena were out for a walk enjoying the fresh air, and greeted him as they passed: 'Good morning'.

He acknowledged them with a friendly nod and engaged them in conversation.

'Excuse me ladies, would you mind telling me if Jayne Jordan and her boy are still living here?'

'But of course! Jayne and James are the heart and soul of The Folly. Don't know what we'd do without them. You must be a friend from Dublin. Isn't it great news about the wedding? It won't be long now till the big day.'

Jack bade them farewell and headed towards the house, his mind now racing with the new information he had acquired.

'Wedding indeed. We'll see about that,' he thought. It never suited Jack when things didn't go his way. He realised he must tread warily and get his facts straight before he approached Jayne.

By now it was almost lunchtime. He went to the reception desk and as subtly as possible ascertained if Jayne would be at the hotel today. Aine Sharkey was filling in at the desk for a few hours. She told him it was unlikely that Jayne would be over from her cottage in the stable yard until evening.

'In fact,' she said, 'I'll be going over to take care of Jack when I'm finished here. I'm his nanny.' Jack took note of this and headed into the bar, where making himself comfortable, he ordered lunch. And there he sat, watching the comings and goings of the guests for several hours.

Chapter 29

Later that afternoon, unknown to her, Jack spotted Jayne coming into the hotel. He slipped out into the garden and made his way to the stable yard, presuming it was somewhere behind the main house. It was a bright May day and the gardens looked magnificent. He followed a path, which he thought would lead him in the correct direction, but he ended up very close to Magdalena's villa. Its size and design fascinated him. 'These people are not short of a few bob!' he thought as he made his way nearer to the house.

Magdalena and Beatrice were sitting in the garden having a glass of wine with Arthur who had tracked them down earlier in the day. Seeing Jack and recognising him from earlier, Magdalena waved a greeting and asked him to join them. Jack refused her invitation, politely pleading a pressing engagement. He wanted to bide his time before making himself known to anyone at The Folly. When he reached the stable yard, he found it a hive of activity. Isaac Thorn was busy sorting out plants which he had brought from the garden centre. He was in animated conversation with Tony and Peter, just returned home from an afternoon at the beach.

'We do like to keep our tans topped up', Peter was saying to Prof. Isaac. Jack made his way to the other cottage, which he presumed must be Jayne's. Aine Sharkey looked pleased, if a little surprised to see Jack again when she opened the door to him.

'I'm afraid you've missed Jayne,' she explained, 'but you'll catch her at the hotel if you go back now. She's not long gone.'

Jack spotted a small boy, hovering around Aine's legs.

'Hello, little man.' James clutched Aine's skirt and stuck his thumb in his mouth.

'Oh! This is James, Jayne's little boy. Haven't you met him before?'

'No, I haven't had that pleasure,' Jack replied, smiling at the child.

'Say hello to the nice man, James.' Aine encouraged James to interact with Jack. 'He's a bit shy, he's not even two yet.'

Jack tussled his hair, thanked Aine and took his leave, saying he would go and find Jayne.

'Who shall I say was looking for her?' Aine called after him as he left the yard but Jack didn't reply.

Several days later, Jayne received a letter. It was unusual to get a handwritten letter in the post, what with social media, texting and email, the scripted missive was rare. She opened the envelope and took out the single sheet of vellum. Staring at it, she moved slowly towards the nearest chair and sat down. Shock, amazement and fear gripped her, as she read Jack's message. James was his son and he now wanted to be involved in his life. He had included his phone number, email address, or 'you can contact me here at home'. Things had obviously changed, if it was kosher for her to have anything to do with the Dublin house. At the time of her pregnancy, his biggest fear was that Vanessa would find out about her or the baby. Jayne sat motionless, staring at the letter, her brain numb. She couldn't even begin to think what to do. The situation was unimaginably complex and she was in the original Catch 22. Stuffing the letter into her pocket, she remained sitting staring into space. A while later, suddenly remembering she was due up at the hotel to look after Eddie and Lizzy, she jumped up, grabbed her coat and made for the door. Panic gripped her as she left the cottage, so going back indoors, she phoned Sandra O'Leary asking her to check the ladies and tell them she was delayed but on her way.

'Are you OK, Jayne?' Sandra enquired, sensing the tension in her voice.

'Yes, yes I'm fine.' She took a deep breath: 'Well no actually I'm not at all fine. I've had a terrible shock.'

'Oh God!' Sandra exclaimed, 'Is James alright?'

'Yes, he's fine, he's in the park with Aine.'

'Look, get yourself up here, we'll calm you down and see if I can help. I'll see the ladies and make sure they're OK.'

Jayne thanked Sandra, and got ready to go out. Even speaking to her friend had broken the spell that the shock of getting the letter caused.

On his return from Scotland and finding his planned move into Magdalena's house aborted, Arthur moved in with Jayne until Marcus returned from the States in about a week. After meeting Beatrice a second time he agreed with Jayne she really was a nice woman. Certainly she and Magdalena had struck up a friendship and as Arthur later declared to Jayne: 'Magdalena does not take prisoners'.

Sandra O'Leary suggested he take one of the holiday guest suites, at a special rate, until it was needed. This didn't appeal to Arthur, who wanted a more permanent arrangement in Crannagh. He decided to check out apartments in the village, to put a few miles between himself, the hotel and its residents. He liked them all, but he was an independent man and not used to such close proximity to other people. This way he could have companionship when he wanted it, see his daughter and grandson often but lead his own private life.

The pub and the post office seemed to be the centres of information in the village but Arthur had no intention of discussing any of his business with 'that nosey old bitch of a postmistress'. So he went to the pub and asked Tom and Brigid Mackey about local accommodation. By late afternoon, Arthur had rented a well-appointed apartment on the outskirts of Crannagh, overlooking the river. He could move in within days and was delighted going back to the stable yard, to tell Jayne his news. He was surprised and disappointed at her lack of interest or enthusiasm when he told her about the apartment. She seemed so distracted and tense that he began to doubt his decision to move to Ireland.

'Is everything alright?' he asked gently. 'You were in great form when I left this morning, but now you seem miserable. Is there something wrong with James?'

'It's not James, Dad, it's me.'

After speaking to Sandra, she had a clearer view of the situation. It was good to talk it through with someone who didn't have preconceptions about Jack, their affair or James's birth. On hearing Jayne's story, Sandra put two and two together, realising the 'tall, dark stranger', to quote Aine, who had come supposedly looking for Jayne, was Jack Redmond. Sandra was quite pragmatic about it all and Jayne agreed with her. She now had to explain her dilemma to Arthur, telling him about the letter and Jack's visit to The Folly a few days earlier. Arthur also reacted when he heard this.

'Good God! So that's who that was.'

'What are you talking about, Dad?'

'He came walking by Magdalena's garden and we just said hello. No idea who he was, of course. Sneaky bastard! It had to be him, spying.'

Only for the seriousness of the situation, Jayne would have found Arthur's reaction funny and almost giggled but got back to telling her story.

'And so you see, Jack is James's father, and I have no right to keep them apart. If you think about it Dad, that is exactly what my grandmother did to us, you and me.'

She went up to Arthur and threw her arms around him. 'To think I almost lost you altogether is unbearable, not to mention Jess and George. I could never do that to James.'

Arthur held her close as she continued: 'And as well as that, James has two sisters. I'm so afraid how it will affect all our lives. I'm glad Marcus is away just now. It gives me time to think.'

'You must tell Marcus everything you're going to do Jayne,' Arthur interjected, hating to interfere but knowing he must warn her about the risk of hurting her future husband.

'I know. I know,' she replied. 'Just not yet.'

Chapter 30

James's first meeting with his father was to take place within a few days. Jayne was pleasantly surprised to find Jack was agreeable about laying down ground rules regarding time with his son. She found the courage to phone him, explaining that James was not used to being away from his familiar surroundings and people he knew.

'That's fine, Jayne, I understand. I can come to Wicklow for our first visit, we can all spend time together and perhaps next time you can bring him to Dublin.'

Although she knew how manipulative Jack could be, she agreed. She spoke to Sarah, again expecting a critical reaction but she too realised this was about father and son. She told Jayne she would help any way she could at the Dublin end.

'Oh, thanks so much, Sarah. Perhaps we could stay with you when we come up to the city.'

'Of course you can,' Sarah replied enthusiastically. 'But just remember, this is Jack you're dealing with. So stay on your guard.'

On the appointed day, at the appointed time, Jack arrived at the cottage. Jayne was busy baking bread and making soup in the kitchen. Marcus was due home the next day and knowing how busy the day would be, she wanted to have lunch prepared. The smell of baking and homemade soup wafted through the house, when Jayne opened the door.

'Well, well, look at you, lovely as ever and not a day older,' Jack beamed at her. 'Yum, something smells good,' he added.

'Oh, hi, it's you,' she replied, determined to appear cool. 'It's for Marcus, he's coming home tomorrow,' she added, putting emphasis on 'home'.

'Marcus, home?' Jack feigned surprise.

'Yes, Marcus my partner. We're getting married soon.'

'That's nice,' Jack replied with little enthusiasm. 'Now, where's my boy?'

Jayne cringed at the mention of 'my boy'. This was not going to be easy but she was glad Marcus was away and today's visit, at least, would be over by the time he got back.

James was playing with his toys on the sitting room floor and paid no heed to the visitor when he first entered the room. Jack had the good sense to approach him quietly, without a fuss. The three sat together on the floor and eventually James was happy to let his father join in the game. Jayne slipped back out to the kitchen, watching from the doorway. She had mixed emotions seeing father and son sitting together and was shocked she felt possessive and a bit jealous. But then she was glad James was so relaxed with Jack.

It was a cloudy morning, but by midday the drizzle had stopped, the clouds had broken and the sun shone. Jack suggested going to the park to let James play on the swings. 'We can have lunch in the village, before I head off.' Jayne was relieved he wasn't staying the whole day, she was stressed and displaced enough already.

Later on, after James had played on the swings and the seesaw, they headed to The Tearooms for lunch. Jack was full of enthusiasm: 'Hey, little man, I'll have to get a swing for you in my garden. Wouldn't you like that?' and he tickled his tummy. James giggled. Jayne frowned. The thought of them together in Dublin without her, was disturbing. She said nothing. At least for the first few visits they'd agreed she would go with him.

Just as Jayne was sitting in the sun in the village, Marcus had finished his business earlier than expected and was driving out of Dublin. He loved when he left the city behind and saw the Wicklow hills and the sea. As soon as he passed the Sugar Loaf, he knew he was home. After every trip to the States, he was delighted and excited to be going back to Jayne and James. He knew he was a lucky man. As always, he had lots of gifts for them and was looking forward to seeing the expression on the little fellow's face when he saw his new toys. In the early afternoon, he drove through the village on his way to The Folly. Spotting Jayne sitting outside the café he decided to park and walk back to surprise her. Making his way up the street he saw Jack and presumed he was there on business to do with the the hotel.

James saw him first and climbed from his chair into his arms as Marcus bent down and gave Jayne a peck on the cheek.

She looked at him in astonishment and stammered: 'But you're not meant to be home until tomorrow.'

'Finished early so thought I'd surprise you,' he replied. Then looking at Jack, he smiled and held out his hand: 'Hello there, nice to see you. I'm Marcus, Jayne's partner.'

Without hesitation Jack shook his hand and said: 'And I'm James's father. Nice to see you too.'

'But Jayne, why did you do that? How could you have let that happen? You never even told me what was going on.' Back in the cottage, Marcus was distraught. No amount of cajoling, pleading, explaining, made any difference.

'Please listen to me,' begged Jayne almost crying with misery and frustration. 'I love you Marcus; James loves you. Jack makes no difference to that.'

Marcus shook his head. 'It's because I love you, Jayne, and because I look on James as my son, it's because of that I can't deal with this situation. If I didn't care so much, it wouldn't hurt, it wouldn't matter. You are my family, and now I've lost you.'

'Of course you haven't lost us. Jack is his father, for God's sake, he's entitled to see his child.'

At this point, Marcus stood up, and looking directly at Jayne declared: 'Until today, you called me James's Dad. Until you arranged to meet that man, behind my back and change everything, I was James's Dad.' Marcus looked exhausted and angry. He had not slept for over 24 hours.

'Marcus, please try to understand. I do not have the right to keep a child and his biological father apart. It would be so wrong. James would never forgive me.'

Looking at her sadly, Marcus put his hand on her shoulder, 'You just don't get it Jayne, do you, you don't understand. I know what you're saying is true and right, but I can't live with it. I can't share you and James with another man.'

With that, as Jayne started to reply, he put his finger to her lips and stopped her, 'No more arguing Jayne, I'm exhausted', and he left the kitchen to sleep in the guest bedroom.

When Jayne woke in the morning from a very troubled and broken sleep, Marcus was gone.

PART 4

Ten months later

Chapter 31

It was St Patrick's Day. The long winter was beginning to give way to brighter days, with the early spring flowers giving life and colour to the landscape and gardens. A smattering of snow still topped the mountains around Wicklow. At Finn's Folly life went on at its usual easy pace. Arthur and Beatrice accepted Magdalena's invitation to join her in Dublin for the festivities. She had spent a couple of weeks at the Shelbourne and was delighted they agreed to come. Beatrice was fascinated when she heard about the parade, the street theatre, and all the activities that were scheduled for the week.

'I can't believe it goes on for a whole week. How Irish. Let's get going.'

Donned in a bright green designer coat and hat she set off with Arthur who had grown to really like and enjoy this zany woman. Jayne had been invited also, but she declined, to help out at the hotel during the busy holiday week. They offered to bring James to Dublin with them as he was scheduled to spend time with his father.

'That would be a great help, thanks. But Dad,' she gave Arthur a stern look, 'no funny business with Jack. Try not to have a go at him. Just hand James over and smile...please.'

Arthur was still furious about Jack's reappearance at The Folly the previous summer.

'I detest that smarmy, sneaky, underhand little snake,' he declared. 'Barging in here as if he owns the place. Showing no respect for you or your son's life.'

He desisted from saying, 'I warned you,' when Jayne admitted she allowed Jack's visit to Crannagh without informing Marcus.

'And he was sneaking around, sussing us all out, days before that. Despicable man.'

Jayne had little to say. At the time she was heartbroken about Marcus's sudden departure. She couldn't believe how badly she had hurt him. The sadness in his eyes and his broken appearance still haunted her. She missed him more, rather than less, as time went by. She had written to him several times, using his business address as she didn't have any other but he never replied. She suspected her letters never reached him. It made it harder that she didn't even know where he was. It seemed a very long time since that fateful day when Jack met Marcus. But life at The Folly continued as normal. When asked about Marcus she explained the wedding was postponed as he had to return to the States urgently. Only Arthur and her close friends knew the real story.

Her relationship with Jack, despite his efforts to have it otherwise, remained formal and distant. She facilitated James's visits to Dublin and by now was happy enough to leave him there for a few days at a time. She couldn't deny that he was a caring father. James loved his sisters, Megan and Sam (short for Samantha), and they loved him back. Vanessa overcame her initial high dudgeon about James and accepted him into the family. She wasn't often involved but it helped when she was. All in all, the arrangements worked well.

Ten months on the residents at Finn's Folly had settled in and after some initial hesitation seemed to have formed friendships and in general tolerated each other surprisingly well. Tony and Peter set up a supper club with the Professor and Matilda and hosted several enjoyable evenings in the stable yard. Jayne was always invited, as their nearest neighbour, and she found, particularly after Marcus left, that their company helped to keep her mood buoyed up. Isaac and his wife took over the running of the kitchen garden, insuring a constant supply of fresh fruit and vegetables for the hotel and cottages. Sandra hired a young man from the village to help. During the autumn the vegetables were picked and frozen to see them through the winter. The fruit also was collected and laid carefully on shelves in the cold store. This hard work, which the Thorns thoroughly enjoyed, subsidised their rent. They were more than happy with the arrangement, being keen gardeners and cooks.

Tony and Peter made full use of the garden, collecting the vegetables, herbs and fresh fruit whenever they needed them. During the dreary winter months the boys became really interested in making preserves, jams, jellies, chutneys. These were firm favourites in the hotel kitchen and Ricardo, the chef, was so impressed with their produce he suggested selling them to the hotel guests. Tony and Peter were delighted and worked like beavers to set up their new business. The hotel restaurant was now a popular venue with a loyal, regular clientele from the village and the environs.

At Christmas that first year, a number of outside guests joined the residents and the festive season was memorable, filled with good food, good wine and lots of entertainment. Mary Forde largely kept herself to herself since arriving in May but surprised the others with her wonderful soprano voice.

'Well,' said Tony, 'that was a well-kept secret.'

She was pleased to take part in the festivities, it broke the ice for her. She joined the supper club and helped produce the preserves. Her OCD had improved remarkably since the stresses and responsibility of managing her own home had been lifted from her shoulders. She could now handle her rituals without letting them interfere with her day-to-day life. She was so happy that her personality became quite outgoing and charming. Of course, due to her obsessive nature, she was extremely organised and tidy. Tony and Peter were thrilled with this and encouraged her involvement in their business.

During the gloomy months of October and November Dame Beatrice suggested afternoon ballroom dance classes. She was a stern but wonderful teacher, imparting her own superb talents as best she could to her unlikely pupils. Many people from the area joined the classes and these eventually evolved into a tea dance held once a week in the drawing room. Colin Smyth was an avid follower of the new dance culture at the Folly, attending every class and tea dance without fail. His enthusiasm, if not his talent, was infectious and before long Margaret, a bit of a loner, was as involved as her husband. With the drawing room carpet rolled back, the music playing and the flicker of candle light on the dark evenings, it made a happy, companionable sight and any onlooker could not resist getting involved.

After Christmas and the New Year, during the bitterly cold days of January a flu virus hit the country. There were health warnings on radio and television, but despite taking all the recommended precautions and despite having the flu vaccine, several of the residents fell victim to the nasty illness. Jayne's nursing skills were now greatly in demand. Lizzy and Edie became very unwell, as did Eve Langton and Major Thompson but after weeks of care, Edie made a good recovery. Lizzy, being older and frailer, developed pneumonia and was confined to bed for many more weeks. Eve was also severely hit by the bug, having built up little resistance to these viruses while living in Texas. The Major was so ill he was admitted to hospital and needed care in a convalescent home after his discharge. Jayne visited him regularly as he improved little by little. The same could not be said for Lizzy. Dr Langton discussed admitting her to the hospital, but Edie insisted she stay at home with as much nursing care as needed and a private nurse was hired. Jayne helped and spent as much time as possible with the two ladies whom she had grown to love dearly.

During her illness, Eve became close to Jayne, spending many long hours together sharing confidences. Eve was tempted to confide the dark secret about her husband on death row to Jayne but had never done so.

After Arthur, James and Beatrice left for Dublin on St Patrick's Day morning, Jayne made her way to Eve's apartment. She wanted to ask her advice.

Chapter 32

The night Marcus left The Folly he looked in on the sleeping baby and his mother to say his goodbyes then drove straight to the city. He had booked a flight to the States next morning and checking into an airport hotel, tried to sleep. His mind was a jumble of emotion and exhaustion, his fevered brain racing. He was heartbroken, sad and angry, but worst of all, jealous. Sleep eluded him and he lay, tossing and turning in the comfortable bed, but the dreariness of the ubiquitous beige and brown of the hotel bedroom only deepened his gloom. He was so sleep deprived he was almost giddy. By dawn he had fairly well emptied the hotel mini bar in an effort to ease his mind and relax. Now he was anxious and inebriated. Being aware of the risk he might not be allowed to fly if drunk, Marcus managed to smarten himself up, and downing numerous cups of black coffee, acted almost normally. Sitting in a window seat on the aeroplane he drank some more and then eventually through sheer exhaustion and alcohol fell asleep.

Summer in Detroit was hot and humid. Marcus planned to rent or sell his apartment but fortunately had not yet done so. Arriving back now, he couldn't bear to be alone. Against his better judgement he headed into the city and went drinking again. This developed into the norm over the next few months. Despite the efforts of friends and company colleagues, Marcus neglected his work and his health. Louisa made occasional visits to her son and was bewildered and worried by his condition and his self-destructive behaviour. Kevin Hunt, his business partner, failed miserably to get through to him. When told the company was suffering financially and employee morale was low, Marcus merely off, telling him he didn't care. This was so out of character for Marcus, usually diligent and loyal to all his friends and colleagues, Kevin believed he was depressed. Dee, Kevin's wife, a long-time friend and confidante, also failed to make any impression on him.

'Marco! Why are you like this? We are all so worried about you. Please talk to me.'

It did no good, he wouldn't even consider going to see a therapist or a doctor. After a time they left him alone. Marcus continued to drink.

It was dusk on a cold night in early December when fate took control of Marcus's problem. He left home shortly after lunchtime and took his car into the city. This was unusual, as although his drinking was out of control, he had always been serious about the evil of drink driving and decided to leave his car in a city car park and catch the bus home. As it happened, there was an industrial dispute in the Detroit Bus And Rail Company, which had disrupted schedules for months. Coming up to the festive season the workers and unions upped their action. On this particular evening there was a go slow with queues of disgruntled passengers waiting in the cold; the taxis were busy. Marcus was now full of drink and decided to drive home.

Driving along the busy thoroughfare, he became more and more impatient. It was twilight, that time of day when the human form takes on the appearance of shadows and sprites. Reaching the open road, he headed at speed in the direction of home. Coming to a pedestrian crossing he didn't notice a young mother with an infant in a buggy start to cross. He jammed on the brakes, bringing the car to a screeching halt, almost out of control. There was a look of terror in the woman's eyes, as she stood directly in his path. He had missed hitting her and her child by a hair's breadth. She continued on her way. Marcus was horrified, shaking from head to toe. Slowly he drove off, went on his way only to be stopped at a road block, not more than a mile from his apartment. He was breathalysed, failed miserably and was hauled off to the police station. A night in the cells of a downtown Detroit police precinct was not only sobering but quite terrifying. Hardened criminals mixed with drunks and hobos. Men in shackles, shouting abuse at the officers, drug addicts and drunks, roaring, screeching and vomiting. It was a scene from hell. Marcus was searched and humiliated being relieved of his shoe laces and belt and seeing his personal belongings being put in a transparent plastic bag, his watch, his wallet, his keys, his phone. Asked about his statutory phone call, he realised there was no one he wanted to see, while in this awful place. Luckily he was put in a single cell. The young policeman who held him tightly by the arm, shoved him in the door and adding to his humiliation snarled: 'Now, no trouble out of you, asshole!'

All through the night, Marcus agonised over the fact that he so nearly killed that innocent young woman and her baby, let alone all the collateral damage, had he hit them. Her terrified expression as she stared right into his eyes through the windscreen would haunt him forever. For the first time since leaving Ireland he was knocked out of his self-pitying mode, and saw life as it is, a series of events, some of which we can shape and many of which we can do nothing about. It's a matter of dealing with what comes your way, be it good or bad. Marcus knew he was the cause of tonight's terrible events and swore that he would put things right. Through the long hours till dawn he thought of all the people he had hurt: Kevin, Dee, all his workmates, his mother, his best friend Michael. Things had to change, and only he could do it. Losing Jayne and James was a heartache but Jack had every right to see his own son. How stupid he had been to presume Jayne would choose him over her child's father.

In the morning, nursing a shocking hangover and deeply hurt pride but with a much clearer view of his life, Marcus was released and advised to get a lawyer to represent him in court. His hearing would come up shortly. The most likely outcome was a minimum of one year off the road or maybe two, considering his extremely high blood alcohol level the previous night. A liaison officer told him he would probably have to go to addiction counselling, to deal with his drinking problem. Marcus was horrified. It had never dawned on him that he had 'a problem'. It more or less all panned out as predicted. By late January Marcus was attending a counsellor weekly and had parted with a hefty sum of money in a fine. His licence was suspended for twelve months. He settled down after it all happened and applied himself to work and to renewing old friendships. He had a lot of apologies to make. In many ways he was lucky. He could have the death of the young mother and baby on his conscience and be serving a long jail sentence had things happened differently. It was almost as if he had been given a second chance and he was determined to get himself back on track.

Christmas and New Year holiday was a quiet affair spent with his mother and his sister Abigail, who had travelled home from Cape Town for the holiday. Louisa confided to Abigail that she was extremely worried about Marcus.

'Ever since he returned from Ireland, that wretched place,' she declared angrily, 'he has been behaving most peculiarly. He tells me very little, but I gather it's to do with that girl he met.'

'Do you know her, mother? Do you know her name?' Abigail was curious because Marcus had spoken to her of a girl in Ireland and something about a child and his father. It was all very vague almost as if he didn't want her to know about it but couldn't keep it to himself. She didn't want to push him to tell her more in case he dried up altogether. She suspected her brother had a broken heart and since returning to Detroit had been suffering from depression. Michael, his childhood friend, agreed with her.

'He's a different person whatever has happened. But he made great strides forward in the past six weeks or so. I think he's attending a counsellor.'

Abigail did not know what to do. She hated seeing Marcus like this, and knowing that his relationship with their mother was very fraught, she didn't want to leave for home without doing something.

'Would you like to come and spend some time in Cape Town? It would be a complete change, so different to here and to Ireland too, I'm sure. Please think about it.'

Marcus followed his sister to South Africa three weeks later.

Chapter 33

When she returned from visiting Eve Langton on St Patrick's Day morning, Jayne searched for Abigail's address, phone number, email, any way to get in touch with her would do. Confiding her true feelings for Marcus to Eve and describing her misery since he left, Eve advised her to keep up her efforts to contact him.

'You'll always regret it if you don't find out where he is and how he is. It sounds to me as though you two are supposed to be together.' She added: 'At least do your best, you can't do more than that.'

All Abigail's contact details must have been on Marcus's computer and Jayne almost gave up but then decided to take the bull by the horns and contact Louisa. Since the time of her disastrous visit to Crannagh her number was in Jayne's phonebook. Allowing for the time difference she decided to call Louisa later that evening. She didn't expect a friendly reception but thought it better if she didn't ring at some ungodly hour.

At the sound of Louisa's voice Jayne almost panicked and hung up but she managed to say hello and introduce herself. She was correct in thinking she wouldn't receive a great welcome as Louisa said sharply:

'What do you want?'

The indignation Jayne felt at being spoken to so rudely, gave her more courage. 'I want to contact Marcus and would appreciate if you'd give me his address.'

There was a momentary silence just long enough for Jayne to realise Louisa was not going to cooperate easily.

'He's not here. He's gone away.'

'But surely you know where he is?' Jayne persisted.

'Maybe.' Louisa replied. There was another pause, longer this time.

Jayne became impatient and annoyed with this awkward woman who seemed to make trouble wherever she went and enjoyed it.

'Look, Louisa, I just want to talk to Marcus. He and I were very close. I miss him and I worry about him.'

Another pause and then: 'He's in South Africa. He's staying with his sister in Cape Town.' She called out Abigail's address and phone number.

'Thank you so much, Louisa. This means a lot to me.'

'I gave it to you for Marcus's sake not yours. I think he misses you too. Now goodbye.'

She ended the call before Jayne could say another word. She had got the information that she wanted so badly and that was all that mattered to her.

Later that day, Eve was delighted when Edie and Lizzy invited her to their suite for tea. She hadn't budged since being laid low with the flu and suspected that this was the ladies' first social interaction also. Jayne went straight over to them as soon as she finished on the phone to Louisa and not wanting to do anything behind their backs, told them of her brief but fruitful phone call to their half-sister. Lizzy looked disgusted but was now too frail to waste her energy giving out. Edie was fascinated and wanted to know had Louisa made any reference to them or The Folly. Hearing what she said and how rude she was to Jayne, she remarked with disdain that she 'had no interest in that selfish woman', but was glad she disclosed Marcus's whereabouts.

When Eve arrived, they ordered afternoon tea from the kitchen and settled down for a good chat. Jayne filled them in on her plan to contact Abigail, and Edie looked surprised but pleased.

'So, my dear, you are off on an adventure to find Marcus. How exciting.'

'And how romantic,' Eve added with enthusiasm.

'Well I'm glad you're going to South Africa and not America. You won't run the risk of meeting that awful Louisa.' Lizzy was still unforgiving and still capable of the bitter word.

'Eh, ladies, not so fast. I have an address that's all. I might not find Marcus or I might not be welcome.' She planned to ring Abigail as soon as she was home that evening. 'I'll let you know what happens when I contact them in Cape Town.'

Jayne left Eve chatting with the sisters and went to help in the hotel. She was excited and encouraged that Louisa said Marcus missed her. She reckoned that was one of the first positive comments she had ever heard Louisa utter.

St Patrick's Day marked the start of the holiday weekends in the year and the hotel was buzzing. The restaurant was fully booked for dinner and Ricardo was busy with his staff, preparing a menu that lent atmosphere to the national occasion. Topping the bill, on the menu, was Irish ham, potatoes and cabbage, with a twist.

'Sounds boring to me!' Sandra complained.

It turned out to be a delicious, sophisticated dish, the twist making it a gourmet experience. Mary Forde, Peter and Tony joined Colin and Margaret Smyth for the occasion. They were a fascinating group to behold, their friendship apparent to all the visitors dining that evening, adding to the warmth of the atmosphere.

'What a pity we can't have a dance,' Peter remarked, but unknown to them all, after dinner, a trad band was lined up to play in the drawing room. Needless to say, dancing followed.

Mary Forde was a surprise package. From her solitary and shy beginnings she had blossomed into a bright flower. No one was more amazed by this transformation, than her. She woke up each morning happy and looking forward to the day ahead. The days when she was controlled and deeply distressed by her obsessive compulsive disorder with its strict, restraining rituals, its guilt provoking mind-set, its fear, anxiety and panic attacks, were behind her. She was liberated, happy and often experienced a childlike excitement over simple events, like today's celebration. From early morning, she had looked forward to her evening out with Peter and Tony. Being preoccupied with neurotic rituals her appearance used never take precedence. As a result, although she had the potential to be a good-looking woman, she was dull, her dress sense dowdy, her dark brown hair peppered with grey. She was slim, but wore unflattering clothes rendering her rather shapeless. Not anymore! Over the weeks and months since living at Finn's Folly she made trips to the shops in Dublin and in Kildare Village, accumulating a wardrobe of stylish garments. The boys, or at least one of them, often accompanied her and she found their taste and advice helpful. Peter particularly enjoyed these trips and was not at all shy to give his opinion.

'Your hair needs to be done,' he declared, on one occasion or: 'What about having your nails done?'

Mary would not be seen with a grey hair, it was now gleaming auburn with copper streaks and she looked years younger. Her manicured hands always boasted perfectly painted nails, in colours complementing her outfit of the day.

And so she was on that St Patrick's night, she looked a picture in a bright blue silk dress and the high-heeled shoes she had also taken to wearing recently, relegating her chunky, flat walking shoes to the cloak cupboard to be used for that purpose solely. Dancing with Peter, Tony and Colin, laughing and joking, she caught Patrick Fogarty's eye. He was genuinely upset at Astrid's death and hadn't noticed any woman since. Stasia had made her move at what she thought would be a good time, offering him sympathy and solace, but he dismissed her attentions, not liking the woman or her behaviour. He came for dinner at the hotel with Tom and Brigid Mackey, who were now waltzing their way around the drawing room. Patrick approached Mary as she sat down after a foxtrot with Tony and asked if she would honour him with the next dance. Mary blushed, surprised by this stranger's attention. But she was delighted and danced with Patrick for the remainder of the evening, only taking a break for a drink at the bar.

As the evening was drawing to a close, Eve Langton popped in to see if Jayne was around.

'She was here earlier,' Margaret Smyth told her. 'We had a good chat, but she left early. She had some important business to attend to.'

Eve suspected that she knew what that business was.

Jayne checked carefully she had disconnected her phone and then exclaimed as she punched the air: 'Yes! Yes! Yes!' She had not received a cold reception from Abigail, as she feared, but Marcus's sister was thrilled to hear from her.

'You have no idea how many times I've thought about calling you recently,' Abigail told Jayne. 'I have been so worried about Marcus. He has only begun to show signs of recovering from his breakdown but I know he's still terribly unhappy.' She went on to tell Jayne she had coaxed Marcus to come to South Africa with her.

'You probably know how difficult our mother can be. Marcus was not improving under her watch. To be fair to mother, she was very worried about him too and was quite happy to see him come to spend time here in Cape Town.'

Jayne was bewildered when Abigail went on to tell her none of this was her fault.

'That's life,' she said. 'Of course everything changed when your child's father reappeared. It's understandable that you and he wanted to make a go of it and be a family. Marcus couldn't handle it, he just fell apart.' She told Jayne she wanted to talk to her, to try to understand the situation and then be more help to her brother.

'He is much better now, but he loves you and your son unconditionally, so it is difficult for him to cope with losing you both.'

Jayne was almost speechless, but managed to say hesitantly: 'But... but it's not like that at all. I have never even considered going back to Jack, he's my son's father. I haven't dated anyone since Marcus left.

I can't believe he thought I had. No wonder he left so suddenly. I couldn't understand it. James, my son, sees his father regularly now, and to be honest, I'm happy about that, but I have no feelings for the man. I love Marcus, and only Marcus.' She began to cry but pulled herself together quickly.

'Abigail, I want him to come back so much.'

They talked for another while, both of them now relieved to clear the air.

'Marcus is still very fragile,' Abigail explained. 'I think it best to keep this conversation to ourselves until you meet him.'

'Meet him?' she exclaimed.

'Jayne, will you come to Cape Town to see him? I'll say nothing. It will be a surprise. Please say you will.'

Jayne was overwhelmed. Whatever outcome she had expected from her call to Abigail, it certainly wasn't this.

'Oh, thank you so much Abigail,' she replied. 'I will come, of course I will. Thank you! Thank you!'

'No, thank you Jayne for being so understanding. As agreed, I'll say nothing about your visit. You will have a lot of organising to do, so let me know when it suits you to travel.' Then she added, 'The sooner the better.'

For a short time after the phone call Jayne went around the cottage like a headless chicken. She thought about everything at once. Her instinct was to throw everything to the four winds and leave the next day. She was excited, nervous, anxious, happy, all at once. Her mind was a cauldron of emotions, but most of all she was happy. She knew where Marcus was and was sad to think how he had suffered but now at last she had a chance to sort things out. It was such an enormous sense of relief and as soon as she settled down, following the shock and surprise of recent events, she began to plan her trip.

Chapter 34

Arthur and his two lady friends had a busy day in the city. The streets were alive with music, theatre and the St Patrick's Day Parade. It was a bright day, the sun did shine on and off, but it was chilly. Well bundled up against the cold, Magdalena and Beatrice allowed Arthur to lead the way. Leaving the Shelbourne, they headed down Grafton Street and caught up with the parade in College Green. There they met a fellow American and Magdalena got into conversation with her.

'I'm heading off on a walking tour of the city after this,' she told them. 'Why don't you join me?'

Magdalena hesitated, but before she could protest, the stranger told her that this was no ordinary tour. 'You're in Ireland now,' she laughed. 'This is a tour with a difference.' She went on to explain that at each stage of the walk, the party would go to a local pub and have a drink. 'You actually mean a pub crawl,' Arthur said, amused by the sudden interest shown by Beatrice and Magdalena. 'How about it girls, will we give it a go?' They had a great time, winding up back in Grafton Street and then in Davy Byrne's pub in Duke Street. A little tipsy but in high spirits, they made their way back to the hotel to have something to eat.

'My favorite pub was The Brazen Head, where we went after Christ Church Cathedral. Imagine, it's the oldest pub in Ireland.' Beatrice was fascinated by the city, declaring that she had no idea how beautiful it was or how steeped in history.

Magdalena agreed saying: 'That pub is older than America.'

Later that evening while having dinner, Arthur's phone vibrated in his pocket.

'Excuse me, please ladies, it's Jayne. I don't think she quite trusts me to behave myself where that man's concerned.' He smiled as he left the dining room and went to the foyer to call his daughter back, returning with a puzzled expression.

'Is everything alright?' Magdalena enquired, concerned at how he looked.

'Everything is fine, I think,' Arthur replied. 'Jayne is going to South Africa.'

'South Africa? But why?'

'She's going to meet Marcus.'

Jack was always sorry when it came to the end of James's visit. The St Patrick's Day holiday was drawing to a close and he was bringing him back to Crannagh the next morning. It was a surprise when Jayne phoned and said she would collect James, asking to speak to him.

When Jayne arrived the following morning he was glad to see she was in good humour. At least it seemed there was no great problem to be addressed.

Having explained her situation to Jack, without mentioning Marcus, she asked if he could look after his son for three weeks.

'So you're off on a holiday? Very nice.' She could sense a degree of jealousy in his begrudging attitude but was prepared to overlook it provided he agreed to have their son to stay with him.

'I'll have to work, Jayne. I couldn't take all that time off.'

She knew he was being awkward for the sake of it and expecting this, she had a contingency plan.

'Aine Sharkey is more than happy to help mind him. She can stay in the house if that suits you.'

In fact, Aine had been delighted with the offer, the prospect of a few weeks in the city really appealed to her. Jack agreed and the arrangement was made. Secretly he was pleased at the prospect of having James to stay for a long spell. He always missed him when he returned to his mother.

'When you've made your arrangements, let me know,' he said agreeably. Jayne was happy that James was staying with his father while she was away. She had never left him for more than a few days, but she knew he'd be safe as houses here in Dublin.

The boy was excited arriving at the Shelbourne Hotel, seeing his grandfather with Magdalena and Beatrice. They wanted to hear all about Jayne's forthcoming trip to South Africa, about finding Marcus and her phone encounter with Louisa. She received their full endorsement of her plan and agreed that Abigail sounded like a really kind and caring person.

'It's hard to believe Marcus and Abigail are even related to Louisa, let alone that she's their mother,' Magdalena observed.

Jayne laughed. 'To be honest, I think they take after their grandmother. She sounds like a lovely, gentle person.'

They spent several days together in Dublin. They spoke at length about Jayne's upcoming trip, and all offered help, both financial and in terms of care for the Finn ladies while she was away.

'And you know, if that man doesn't take proper care of James, we can bring him home to Crannagh. We'd love to have him.' Arthur never missed a chance to have a swipe at Jack.

Jayne smiled to herself but said nothing. 'James certainly is a very loved child,' she thought with pleasure.

Magdalena called her aside one evening and handing her an envelope, told her one of her boutique hotels was in South Africa in the Western Cape, along the Garden Route.

'If everything goes well, Jayne and you'd like a holiday with Marcus, just make a reservation and this letter will ensure you are treated as very special guests. And I mean my guests, stay as long as you like.'

Things were getting better.

Back in The Folly, several days later Eve, Edie and Lizzy were delighted to hear Jayne was going to see Marcus, hoping they would be reconciled.

Jayne told them: 'Getting there and meeting him again, just being able to talk to each other and sort this mess out, would be enough for me. Hurting him like that was never even remotely on my agenda. I really want him to know that.' She paused, and then added: 'He may well have moved on from us and Ireland by now. You never can tell how time and circumstances change people and how they feel.'

The ladies nodded in agreement, each secretly hoping this would not be the case and Marcus would come back. They all missed him, especially his aunts who had grown to love him like a son. Finn's Folly had not been the same since he left.

Eve, who was recovered from the flu and had regained her usual energy, assured Jayne that as well as keeping Edie and Lizzy company while she was away, she would visit the Major at the convalescent home. Strong old fellow that he was, he too had started to improve healthwise and was now talking about returning home. 'Hopefully within the next few weeks we'll all be back where we belong.' Edie was looking forward to happier times ahead. Lizzy chuckled at her sister's remark.

'What's so funny, Lizzy?', Edie asked.

'Did you ever think we would have a life so full of people and activity, from old ladies like us to a little fellow like James and every variety of individual in between.'

Edie agreed. 'You're right, you know. We're very lucky. And it all happened by accident, in a way.'

'I have a gut feeling, things will get better.'

'I hope you're right, Lizzy. Now let's have a nice glass of sherry.'

Five days later, Jayne left for Cape Town.

Chapter 35

Easter was early that year, the first weekend in April. Despite the feeling of spring in the air, the bulbs making a colourful show and longer, brighter days, the weather was still cold and windy with April showers bursting from the heavens at regular intervals. On one such morning Mary Forde met Patrick in the village for coffee at The Tearooms. They had spent a lot of time together since the party in The Folly the previous month. Patrick had not been so contented for many years, and it seemed that Mary felt the same way.

'Neither of us are spring chickens,' he said to her gently, his voice hushed, hoping not to be overheard. Stasia had been keeping a keen eye on proceedings during the past few weeks and was horrified to see her chances of catching Patrick ebb away, all because of that odd old one from The Folly. Any bit of gossip was gold dust to her ears.

'Perhaps it sounds premature to you, I do hope not, but I would be very honoured if you would agree to marry me.'

There was a stunned silence. Mary looked shocked and Patrick thought, a bit horrified too.

'Oh dear, I'm so sorry. Really I am, I never meant to offend you Mary. Please forgive me.' He was almost stuttering, he was so distressed at having caused such a reaction.

'Forgive you?' Mary exclaimed when she caught her breath, 'forgive you; oh my dear, dear Patrick, you'll never know how happy you've made me. Of course I'll marry you!'

Patrick grasped her hand and kissed it. His old world chivalry endeared him even more to Mary.

'You see, Mary, I have never in my 62 years felt so relaxed and happy in anyone's company and I don't think we should waste one minute of this valuable time.'

Mary agreed completely and there and then they decided to slip away somewhere abroad to tie the knot. 'We'll tell no one until the deed is done, agreed?'

At that point, Patrick, forever the romantic, produced a little box from his pocket. It contained a beautiful solitaire diamond ring on a delicate chain. Tears brimmed in Mary's eyes as he fastened the chain around her neck.

'Until we get married, I thought you would like to wear it as a symbol of our love and affection.'

One of Stasia's cronies spotted this activity and made her way out of the café down the road to the post office.

'Well, Stasia,' she declared for all to hear, 'there's some right shenanigans going on up there in The Tearooms. That Patrick Fogarty and the one from The Folly are getting very cosy together.'

Despite Stasia's best efforts to get to the bottom of what was going on and all her jealousy and ill will, Patrick and Mary managed to surprise everyone when they arrived back from Paris three weeks later, a married couple.

Eve Langton had been busy since Jayne left for South Africa. She visited the Major regularly, almost daily, and had become very fond of the old fellow. He, for all his talk and stories, seemed to be very much alone in the world. The staff at the convalescent home told Eve that since Jayne left she was his only visitor.

'We see that sometimes when an older person outlives his family and friends. He talks a lot about his army days but you people at Finn's Folly are, in his eyes, his new family.'

When Eve reported this information back to the residents, they were all concerned and some were a little guilty, as they viewed the Major as a self-confident, slightly arrogant man.

'That's probably his way of covering up his insecurities.' They all agreed with Eve.

From then on, Edie, Margaret and Colin, Prof. Thorn, Matilda and the boys visited him regularly. Beatrice, and Magdalena also called a few times, as did Arthur. The Major's mood lifted, and before long so too did his health and he returned home to The Folly.

James was having a great time in Dublin. After a day or two, he was used to the fact that Jayne was away for a while but would be back soon. Time meant little in his child's world and every now and again he and Aine would count how many more sleeps till Mummy comes home. Aine enjoyed her time in the city and was impressed with Jack's devotion to his son. Because of his rather arrogant attitude to life in general he gave the impression of being hard but when it came to James this couldn't be further from the truth. He told Aine he'd like to continue the arrangement of her coming to his home with James, even after Jayne returned. She was chuffed.

By the end of May that year, Mary and Patrick and the Major had all returned to Crannagh.

Chapter 36

When Arthur dropped Jayne at the airport she made her way to departures with some trepidation.

'Next stop London, and then Cape Town, here I come.' She was flying overnight and would touch down just after dawn. To her great relief Abigail was waiting at arrivals. They hadn't met before but somehow knew each other right away.

'I've heard so much about you, I feel I've known you for years,' Abigail commented as they made their way to the car park. The sun was just rising, the mountains, high and rugged silhouetted against the blazing, red sky. The air was balmy with a soft breeze blowing, which was refreshing after many hours on the aircraft. Jayne took a big breath.

'Are you OK?' Abigail enquired.

'Fine, thanks!' Jayne replied, 'I just can't believe I'm actually here at last. I can't wait to see Marcus.' Then realising this might sound rude or somewhat dismissive of Abigail and ungrateful for all her kindness, she added: 'But of course I'm really enjoying meeting you Abigail. Thank you so much for making all the arrangements.'

'I understand how you feel. Of course you're anxious to meet my brother. That's what this is all about.' She gave Jayne a reassuring hug. 'Now let's go and have a good breakfast. It will set us up for the day.'

Driving towards the city, Jayne was taken aback at the sight of mile after mile of townships, shacks where a large proportion of the population lived in poor conditions, with minimal sanitation. She said nothing, not wanting to sound critical of the country, having just arrived. Outside the city, with Table Mountain as the backdrop, they sat outdoors as the sun rose higher in the sky and the warmth of the day increased, enjoying a much appreciated breakfast.

'Airplane food not alone doesn't fill you, it makes you sick.' Jayne laughed, as she scoffed her plate of bacon and eggs, and drank the hot, steaming coffee. They sat looking out over the ocean, Jayne relaxed, and time stood still.

Later that day when Jayne had checked into her hotel which was close to Abigail's home in the southern suburb of Constantia, they sat together in the garden and Abigail explained the situation with Marcus. They both agreed it would be better if Jayne had her own accommodation until she and Marcus talked things over and hopefully had reunited. Since coming to Cape Town his health and mood were greatly improved. He was involved in a city regeneration scheme, allowing him to use his professional skills as an architect but also to do hands-on manual work, 'to get his hands dirty', which he reckoned was the best therapy of all.

'By helping other people, and believe me Jayne these people need help, he is taking his mind off himself. After leaving Ireland he went right downhill, neglecting himself, his work, his health, generally running himself into the ground. He was deeply depressed, but is on his way back now, thank goodness.'

Abigail arranged to collect Jayne for dinner at her house that evening. 'Marcus will be home around six o'clock, you being there will be a huge surprise.'

'A good one, I hope,' Jayne replied nervously.

Chapter 37

Victor Terblanche was the foreman at the site where Marcus worked. A big, friendly, coloured man, Victor kept a tight rein on the regeneration project and on the volunteer workers who arrived from different countries for two weekly stints. The Irish volunteers were a regular bunch, hard workers and hard players too. He was very fond of them. He enjoyed their sense of fun and zany sense of humour. The two men became friendly over the weeks since Marcus arrived in Cape Town. He also liked the Irish connection which certainly gave Marcus an edge when dealing with the volunteers from his adopted land.

'So what brought you here, away from your new-found home?' Victor asked, but didn't follow up on his enquiry when he realised Marcus did not want to discuss it.

'It's a long story, perhaps I'll tell you one day.'

At lunchtime on the day Jayne arrived in South Africa Marcus told Victor he was leaving for the day.

'I have an important meeting. I'll check over the recent drawings and plans at home later. See you tomorrow.'

The site was on the coast overlooking the ocean and there were several beautiful beaches in close proximity. Marcus bought a picnic lunch at the local deli and headed to meet Linda at the nearest one. She was a close friend of Abigail's, a clinical psychologist who had agreed to help Marcus in his recovery. At first he resisted, claiming he was fine again and could cope without help. Soon realising that this was not the case, he agreed to meet Linda who won him over completely with her direct but gentle manner and kind disposition.

They planned to have lunch, followed by a walk with lots of time to talk without interruption.

'What happened to you in Ireland last year was a disaster,' she explained gently. 'You see Marcus, you had a very dysfunctional childhood. In reality you grew up like two separate people. One child was contented and happy, learning excellent life skills from your grandmother. The other child was brought up to be spoiled and indulged, without love, as you knew it in your grandmother's home. You were confused. Thankfully the genuine goodness of your gentle upbringing won through but the confusion remained. You ended up trying to please them all and you were stressed. You then married "your mother". Marissa, the bully, was the final nail in your coffin if you'll forgive the analogy.'

They walked along in companionable silence. Marcus relaxed, his shoes off, feeling the water wash over his feet and the warm sand between his toes. It all made sense but what now, where was he to go from here?

'Well,' Linda continued, 'Jayne came into your life. She, from what you tell me, is the epitome of everything you learned to value from your childhood with your grandmother. She was precious, as was her son, whom you grew to love like your own. The sheer agony of that being taken away from you tipped you over the edge.'

Marcus was amazed at this exposé of himself. The more he thought about it, the more he understood and agreed with Linda's analysis.

Arriving home that evening he had a lot to think about and a lot of plans to make. He had arranged to meet Linda again the following week. Nothing could have prepared him for the complete shock when he saw Jayne. She approached him, gave him a peck on the cheek and a hug. Marcus was speechless.

At first he was reticent and somewhat withdrawn, but as time went by, he became more relaxed and began to enjoy their time together. Jayne explained her situation at home, her formal, business-like relationship with Jack, her continuing love for Marcus. The next few weeks passed quietly with Marcus and Jayne spending every available hour together. 'No one was ever going to take your place. All the misunderstanding between us happened because I was afraid of upsetting you and losing you. Marcus, I am so sorry for hurting you; I never meant to. I was a coward, I should have told you straight away what was going on. Please forgive me. I can be such a fool.'

Marcus assured her it was just as much his fault. 'I should have listened to you, Jayne. I should have understood. It's me who should be apologising, not you.'

They travelled along the coast for several days, stopping off at towns along the way and ended up in Wilderness, a beautiful coastal village boasting magnificent scenery, a lagoon, miles and miles of unspoiled sandy beaches set against a backdrop of majestic mountains. Magdalena's hotel was here, an old world, Cape Dutch style manor house, restored with precision and perfection to its former glory. Marcus and Jayne were welcomed with all the attention afforded to their most prestigious guests. They spent their days walking and swimming, lying in the sunshine, drinking wine and eating wonderful food, and their nights lying together in the comfort of each other's arms, contented after making love. Life was timeless.

When the time came to return to Cape Town it was like a bubble had burst.

'What now?' Jayne asked as they neared the city. 'Where do we go from here?'

Marcus was silent and became withdrawn again.

'I must stay here, Jayne. I'm not ready to leave or change my life again. Besides, I'd be no good to you the way I am. I have a long way to go yet.'

Jayne did not expect this response and was bitterly disappointed but remembering her warning to Eve and Edie back home that Marcus might have changed, she knew in her heart this could happen. He had no right, he tried to explain, to take over her life and James's life while in no fit state to look after himself, let alone anyone else.

'But,' she pleaded, 'I could help you, perhaps we could help each other. That's what love is all about, isn't it?'

'Jayne, I don't even like myself right now. Please don't expect me to share emotions with you that are all muddled up and confused. Basically, my darling girl, I am a mess.'

After many such conversations it dawned on Jayne she was getting nowhere; if anything she was alienating him further. It was not in her nature to be needy and demanding and she hated this happening to her. She gave up and booked her flight home. Abigail was sorry to see her go and waved her off at the airport, promising to keep in touch regularly.

'Don't give up on him Jayne, please. He really loves you.'

A couple of days later, three weeks after leaving Crannagh, Jayne returned home alone.

Chapter 38

In the back of her mind, Sarah always felt that one day, something really wonderful would happen to her. She was a carer, always looking out for friends and family, rarely giving much thought to herself. As a result of the unselfish, happy disposition which selfless people seem to acquire, she was popular with everyone. She was in a state of high excitement when Jayne arrived on her doorstep.

'Oh, Jayne, it's you! Sorry, sorry,' she gave Jayne a welcoming hug: 'That didn't sound very friendly! I've just got a letter from a solicitor and was reading it as the doorbell rang.' She waved a piece of paper in the air, hopping up and down on the spot.

'It's my Aunt Sylvia, well great-aunt really. Oh Jayne, she died a while ago.'

Jayne looked surprised: 'Hardly a cause for celebration, I'd have thought.'

'Oh God, no. Of course not, poor old dear, 94 she was. Didn't look a day of it. Anyway, are you listening? She has just gone and left me €400,000! 400,000!'

Taking Jayne's case from her and dropping it on the floor she grabbed her hands and danced around the room singing: 'I'm rich! I'm rich, rich, rich!'

Jayne laughed with her as they swung around the small sitting room.

'You lucky bitch, Sarah!'

'I know; good old Aunt Sylvia, she's going to change my life.'

Later on when she'd calmed down but still brimming with excitement, Sarah looked at Jayne with a puzzled expression.

'What are you doing here? I thought you were in South Africa.'

'I'm back!'

'Well I can see that. But why and well … no Marcus?'

'No Marcus!' Jayne replied.

It was almost lunchtime and they'd spent the morning talking about all that happened. Jayne was so excited about the inheritance that she didn't feel like going on about herself but Sarah insisted on hearing every last detail about her trip to South Africa. She was astonished to hear of the big change that came over Marcus, his breakdown and new life in Cape Town.

'So he says he can't come back; his life has changed for good! Amazing!' Sarah shook her head knowingly.

'Well he didn't say never, in fact he said, "never say never".' Jayne told Sarah about Marcus's visits to Linda, the psychologist and how she believed his strange, mixed up childhood had damaged him.

'That bloody Louisa, she'd do anyone's head in. Selfish old bat!'

Sarah had no fond memories of Marcus's mother and remembered the mischief she had caused in Crannagh.

'So what's your plan now, Jayne? You surely can't put your life on hold for much longer in the hope that he'll change his mind and come back to Ireland?'

Jayne looked down, refusing to meet her friend's eye.

'Sarah, the awful truth is that I love the man, I want to marry him, so I'll have to give it some time.'

Sarah, putting her arm around her shoulders and giving her a reassuring squeeze, said she understood but didn't really understand any of it. It seemed to her Jayne was the most unfortunate person when it came to men. First Jack and now the elusive Marcus. Even her relationship with her father had been complicated.

'Does anyone know you're here?'

Jayne had left Cape Town early, she'd had enough emotional upset, and wanted to get away.

'I thought I could stay with you for a few days Sarah while they all suppose I'm still in South Africa. It might help to get my feet on the ground before I collect James and head back to Wicklow.'

Hearing this, on top of the good news of her inheritance, delighted Sarah, who promptly arranged some time off work.

'First things first,' she said, smiling broadly at her friend. 'Grafton Street, lunch, wine, and ... shopping.'

Chapter 39

When Jayne left, Marcus was miserable. He knew she felt rejected and badly let down by his reactions but also knew he was doing the right thing. He threw himself into his work, drawing a small wage from the project but donating much more from his private funds. The work was progressing nicely, the houses going up steadily. Many families had already moved into their new homes where they had fresh running water and sanitation facilities beyond their wildest dreams. The great divide between rich and poor bewildered Marcus. All the everyday things like a shower and a lavatory he took for granted all his life were extraordinary luxuries to these people. He worked longer and longer hours, drowning his emotions in work and exhaustion, so much so that Victor Terblanche took him aside one day and asked him what was going on.

'You can't keep this up Marcus, no one can. You take no time for yourself. You'll become unwell.'

Linda also warned he was heading for a breakdown if he didn't slow down.

It was the night of the fire in the township that really pushed Marcus to the brink. After dinner that evening, Victor called to tell him about the fire. Arriving at the site and seeing the destruction and misery, he finally caved in and admitted he could take no more. Anxious and depressed, he agreed to take a break. He headed off to the Transkei, an area on the east coast far away from the bustle of the city, a homeland where people could live native lives and leave their worries and stresses behind. He spent many weeks there and little by little, his body and mind began to recover. He could sleep, eat and laugh. Following long days fishing, walking and swimming, he would fall into bed and sleep the sleep of the just.

Chapter 40

'Oh, by the way,' Sarah said to Jayne, as they sat sipping champagne in the Westbury Hotel cocktail bar, 'Patrick Fogarty and Mary slipped off to Paris while you were away and got married.'

'Married?' Jayne exclaimed. 'I knew they had a bit of a thing going, but married? That's amazing.'

Sarah continued: 'I met Aine Sharkey for coffee a few times while she's been at Jack's, she filled me in on The Folly affairs. Seemingly they're smitten, happy as the proverbial pigs in the proverbial … muck.'

'Well for some,' Jayne muttered.

'What did you say?'

'Oh, nothing important,' Jayne replied, realising she sounded a bit begrudging. She hated the effect Marcus was having on her. She was afraid of becoming self-obsessed.

Jayne changed the subject. 'Speaking of Jack, have you any news from that department?'

Sarah shrugged. 'Maybe it's my imagination, perhaps I'm getting the wrong end of the stick but Aine seems very into Jack. He can do no wrong. It's great really, James is so well looked after by them both. You have no need to worry when you leave him there. Now what about another glass?' Jayne was slightly edgy to hear this news about Jack and Aine. It seemed like the whole world was moving on, leaving her behind. Patrick and Mary getting married, Aine and Jack getting on so well, James fine without her, Sarah becoming rich. She stopped herself, determined not to allow any more self-pity, accepted another drink and raising her glass to Sarah said: 'Here's to you, my best and dearest friend, good luck with your new-found wealth.' They both laughed. Jayne felt better.

A few days later, when Jayne decided she was up to facing the real world, she contacted Jack and arranged to collect James to bring him home to Crannagh. Sarah agreed to drive them down to Wicklow, saying she wanted to see everyone and thought she might put a plan she had in her mind into action. She refused to say anything more about it.

'Just wait and see. Be patient. Nothing might come of it.' Arriving at Jack's house, Jayne had butterflies in her tummy, she was so excited at the thought of seeing James again. It seemed like an eternity since she left him.

Jack opened the door. There was no sign of their son.

'Áine has taken him out for a while.' Jack told her, seeing her surprise that he was not there to greet her. 'I want to have a word with you.'

Telling Sarah she was a little delayed, she went inside. Sarah waited in the car.

'Take a seat. Would you like a tea or coffee?'

He went to the kitchen while Jayne looked around the room. It was filled with toys and children's books. There were paints and crayons spread all over the table and Jayne smiled when she saw James's art work.

Jack returned with the coffee. 'So, how was the holiday? You're admiring our son's artistic masterpieces, I see.'

Jayne was uncomfortable. For the first time since his birth, she was somewhat distanced from James, as though he didn't belong with her anymore. She shook off this feeling, believing it was only because of the long separation and as soon as she saw him, everything would go back to normal.

While they drank their coffee Jack made small talk, telling her all about James's visit, his progress and his antics. Jayne wondered what he really wanted to talk about. Finally he cut to the chase and without ceremony declared: 'I want to share custody of James; I want him to live here with me half of the time.'

Silence, an awkward, shocked silence followed, broken only by the ticking of the clock on the mantelpiece, for what seemed like a long time. Jayne's mind was in turmoil and she went numb as she sat, staring at Jack unable to process the conversation they were having. She wanted to scream and cry and beg Jack not to do this but the terrible reality pierced her heart: she could do nothing to stop it happening.

On the drive back to Crannagh, the girls said little about what had happened. When the time came to leave, James had been truculent and uncooperative.

'I want to stay here with Daddy. Don't let them take me away Daddy, please!' he begged, breaking Jayne's heart. Jack looked smug but explaining that he must go home to 'Mummy's house' for a while, he persuaded him to climb into Sarah's car.

'Don't worry,' he told Jayne, 'kids do this sort of thing when they're separated for a while. It will all be fine when we have our new arrangement up and running. We'll talk soon, and sort things out, alright?'

As they left the city behind and headed into the country James calmed down and fell asleep, exhausted by his tantrum.

Sarah tried to comfort her friend, who was understandably disturbed by her son's reaction on her return.

'Try not to take it to heart Jayne, he's just a child and probably feels a bit mixed up with the comings and goings recently. By the time he's home he'll be happy as Larry again. You wait and see.'

'It's him being mixed up that worries me, it's only going to get worse,' Jayne replied, telling Sarah about the custody issue. 'The older he gets, the more complicated it will be, what with preschool and then primary school. Oh Sarah, it will be a mess.'

'It's early days, he's not three years old yet.'

'Umm,' Jayne was pensive, not convinced, 'Anyway first things first, I'll get home and then sort things out with Jack.'

They drove on in silence, each lost in their own thoughts. Sarah would have loved to share her secret with Jayne, especially now, to distract her from her own problems. However it was all very up in the air and she didn't want to raise their hopes prematurely. When she heard about Patrick and Mary's marriage and their decision to live at Finn's Folly, she thought of Forest Cottage. Situated on the outskirts of Crannagh on the edge of a pine forest, it had been home to Patrick and his parents. When his mother, who outlived his father by many years, passed away, Patrick continued to live there alone. From the first time Sarah laid eyes on it, it became her dream home. Long and low with a thatched roof, in the style of old Irish homesteads of latter years, it was quintessentially traditional. She phoned Patrick, appearing rather pushy but afraid of missing her opportunity to fulfil her dream, asked if he'd consider selling it.

He replied: 'Everything has moved so fast, I haven't had time to think about it. Why not meet me when you're down this way and we'll have a chat.'

Sarah was delighted there was even the remotest chance of making the purchase. Since her first visit to Crannagh and The Folly she loved everything about it. To live close to Jayne would mean the world to her and she believed her friend would think the same way.

Jayne meanwhile, lost in thought, was looking forward to arriving home to her cottage in the stable yard. At least there she felt safe, protected by her friends and her father. They wouldn't be able to solve her problems but they would be there to support and understand. She knew they would be disappointed Marcus did not return with her. At least, she knew she had done her best and she still hoped one day they would be together.

When Patrick told Mary about Sarah's phone call, it set them thinking about their future plans. They had decided to live at Finn's Folly, Mary explaining to her husband how much the move there had helped her conquer her obsessive compulsive disorder.

Patrick confided to her: 'You know, Mary, I've always thought I'd love to retire there and now is my chance. With my savings and pension I'll be comfortable and happy to lead a gentleman's life.'

'So you'll be stuck under my feet all day,' Mary jokingly replied. 'I didn't know I'd signed up for that!'

Whether or not to sell the cottage was the next decision and they agreed it was best to dispose of it with all the responsibilities it incurred.

'Tenants can be a right pain and it would be a shame to leave it unoccupied for too long. It's old and needs tender loving care.'

Patrick was quickly adjusting to the idea of the good life, free of worry.

Later that evening he called Sarah and asked her to meet him for lunch the following day, in the hotel bar.

Arriving home the girls threw open the windows to let in the fresh air. James woke from his sleep and was, as Sarah predicted, in much better form. He was delighted when Arthur arrived to welcome them back and hot on his heels were the Thorns, Peter and Tony.

'We all missed you. You seemed to be gone an age.'

Peter was fussing around and invited them all for an early supper. The excitement of the homecoming was a distraction to Jayne and as they sat chatting in Peter and Tony's cottage, enjoying the glorious aromas of the cooking, she almost forgot her worries about Marcus and Jack. Assuming she would have told him if it was otherwise, Arthur realised Marcus had not returned to Ireland with her and didn't mention his name. He decided he could talk to her later, in private, if she wanted to.

After a delicious supper, Jayne left James in the care of Sarah and Arthur and made her way to the big house to call on the Finn ladies. She was warned over supper Lizzy had not been well during the previous few weeks and often asked for Jayne when she was confused. She received a great welcome but was taken aback to see how weak and fragile Lizzy had become since she last saw her. She took Jayne's hand and gently squeezing it, said how much she'd missed her.

'Everyone was very good to us, especially Eve, but there's no one like you.'

While Jayne was chatting to them telling them all about South Africa, Lizzy nodded off to sleep. She didn't want to disturb them about Marcus, so she said he was very busy working in Cape Town and would probably come to visit in the next few months.

'Tell me, Jayne,' Edie asked gently, 'are you alright?'

'I'm fine,' Jayne replied, knowing Edie realised all was not well.

'You know you can always talk to me. I may be old, but I still remember the traumas of love.'

Jayne smiled, kissed her cheek and promising to bring James to visit the next morning, she went back home.

Sarah met Patrick the next day and was delighted when he told her he would consider selling the cottage. After lunch, they headed into the village to view it. She was enthralled. She always admired the outside when passing but never in her wildest dreams imagined its beauty and character inside. It was impeccably maintained and although very old, bright and cheerful, with beautiful colours and lots of light. The gardens were well tended, with an abundance of early summer blooms. Old trees bordered the property, giving way to the pine forest, with walking trails and a rapidly flowing river. Sarah was overwhelmed and had to hide her enthusiasm, having been warned to negotiate a good price.

'Yes, it's very nice,' she said, ashamed at her understatement. She wanted to declare, at the top of her voice, that she absolutely loved everything about it.

Later she described to Jayne how she had discussed the price and the purchase of the cottage in a very business-like manner.

'Honestly, you'd have thought I'd done this loads of times before. I was quaking, but it worked. Patrick was thrilled too. Said it was the easiest deal he'd ever made.'

They were both so excited they forgot all the troubles of the past few days and sat up into the night discussing Sarah's move to Crannagh.

'You could be here by Christmas, all going well,' Jayne enthused.

Sarah laughed. 'Easy on now; I'll have to keep on my job in Dublin for a while anyway, until I get something down this way. But never mind all that, I'll be here as much as possible. I'm so excited!'

Early the next morning, Sandra O'Leary phoned Jayne to say Lizzy was unwell and asking for her. She went straight to the big house. A few hours later, Lizzy passed away peacefully.

Chapter 41

Lizzy's death cast an air of gloom over The Folly and indeed over the whole village. It was a small community and the Finns had been an important part of it for a long time. Stasia kept her customers well informed about all the activity surrounding the funeral. She gleaned as much information as possible from Patrick when she met him at Mackey's. Her attitude to him was now reserved and stiff, as if she was the woman scorned. But being Stasia, pride would not come between her and local gossip. Patrick told her as little as possible, but Stasia had a way of wangling information out of the most unwilling subject.

'So you're living up there now at The Folly, are you?' she enquired begrudgingly. 'I expect you hear all the news. What happened to the old lady? Was she sick for long or was it sudden?'

Patrick replied with some annoyance: 'Well, she wasn't murdered, if that's what you're getting at, Stasia, she died of natural causes. No Agatha Christie story. She was a very old lady, you know.'

Ignoring his sarcasm Stasia laughed and dropping her defences momentarily, said coquettishly: 'Oh Patrick, you're a terrible man.' Recovering from her momentary lapse she continued her interrogation: 'So, tell me, when will the funeral be?'

Weary of her now, Patrick gathered up his newspaper and glasses, emptied his pint of beer and told her brusquely: 'It will be in the papers.' He left without further conversation.

Much to Edie's surprise, Lizzy left clear instructions about her final resting place. For Lizzy, forever conforming and old fashioned, this decision marked quite a change. During her latter weeks, she wrote letters to several of her close family and friends, leaving them with her solicitor for safe keeping until her death. Reading her sister's letter Edie wondered if she could fulfil Lizzy's last wishes. She loved her older sister; they shared their lives, their concerns and secrets since childhood and she dearly wanted to do what she requested. In Lizzy's familiar, tidy script she read:

My dearest Edie,
You have been my closest and most precious friend and ally all our lives; you made many wise decisions and encouraged me to do the same. With your guidance, we had a happy and carefree life. We missed Dorothea when she left for America but loved Astrid. Our only great sorrow was losing them. I would like, dear Edie, to be cremated when I die and for my ashes to be spread, next to Dorothea's in the woodland in The Folly garden. Also, if you are happy to do so, I would like your ashes, when the time comes, to join us there.

My dear Edie, I will not burden you, at this late stage of your life with an inheritance which you do not need. I had intended to leave my legacy to Astrid. This, not now being possible, I have decided to leave my estate to Jayne, whose goodness to us has been superb. She must accompany you to the reading of my will.

With much love to you, my lovely sister, I bid you farewell and look forward to seeing you in another place one day. From your loving sister,
Lizzy

Taking a deep breath and as tears ran down her face, Edie folded the letter carefully and tucked it away in her pocket. Lizzy's requests were simple and easy to fulfil. Arrangements would be set in place, as soon as she had spoken to the others concerned.

Jayne was busy tidying Lizzy's belonging in The Olivia Suite and Edie noticed she was crying quietly as she went about her work. Edie took her by the arm and leading her to an armchair sat her down to speak to her.

'You were very special to my sister, Jayne. You've shown great devotion to us both, two old ladies whom up to a few years ago you had never even met. Thank you for that.' She gave her a hug and keeping her arm around her, asked Jayne to please continue looking after her.

'I know I seem quite independent but despite my robust health, I need help. I'm getting old and rely on you, Jayne.'

Jayne presumed accompanying Edie to the solicitor's office was part of her duty of care and was surprised, when she was the main subject of the meeting. The solicitor handed her a letter and said they'd continue their conversation when she'd read it. She was shown to a quiet reception room and given a cup of coffee. Jayne asked Edie to stay with her.

'Lizzy was your sister, you must be involved in everything concerning her.'

She read the letter, surprise and bewilderment overcoming her the more she read. Again, tears filled her eyes, an occasional one falling on the pages as she read.

My Dearest Jayne,

My days are now coming to an end. I am an old lady and you, my dear girl, did so much to make my last years happy and contented. I bless the day you arrived with Astrid in The Folly, a naturally caring person, nothing too much trouble for you. Astrid is no longer with us, and you have become my close friend and confidante. I wish to bequeath all my estate to you. My hope is this will help you and your little son to have a happy and less stressful life. You will now be part owner of Finn's Folly and on the board of directors with Edie, Magdalena, and Marcus. You should be secure for life.

There is one thing I wish for you but cannot fulfil; I wish for Marcus's return and your reunion. You belong together. Every day, I wish for this, as I saw the sadness in your eyes. One day, when you least expect it, he will be beside you and the sun will shine for you both again. Believe me Jayne; be patient.

It is with great love to you and your son that I bid you a final farewell and wish you all the happiness that you deserve.
Your loving friend,
Lizzy

Neither Edie nor Jayne could speak. They listened as the solicitor finished his business with them. Then they left his office and went home to The Folly.

Chapter 42

Late in the afternoon of Lizzy's funeral a storm hit the country. It was forecast but much worse than expected with near hurricane force winds and driving rain. These, combined with high tides, led to flooding and electricity blackouts. The east coast was particularly badly affected.

As the funeral party made its way back from the crematorium the skies darkened and black clouds rolled in from the sea. They were almost blown through the front door of Finn's Folly, where Ricardo had a hearty meal ready. Just as they began to eat the lights went out. The generator was running in anticipation of a power failure and so the kitchen could continue functioning to a limited extent. It also lit the emergency lights on the corridors and in the bathrooms. After dinner all the residents gathered around the fire in the bar where Sandra O'Leary had lit plenty of candles. The atmosphere was warm and though tinged with the sadness of the occasion there was an air of companionship. Magdalena sat with Edie, Beatrice and Eve Langton. Edie reminisced about Lizzy, their childhood, their life together in The Folly and the others were happy to listen. Magdalena told Edie she received a letter from Lizzy via her solicitor that morning.

'Would you like to hear what she wrote?'

Edie nodded and Eve and Beatrice made to leave so as not to intrude on a private moment.

'Oh no, please stay. I'm delighted you all knew Lizzy so well. You were her friends. She would want you to be here.'

'And we all loved her, didn't we?' Magdalena added. 'Here, let me read this to you. It is very sweet.'

My dear Magdalena,

When you arrived into our lives at Christmas that year, we were all so afraid of losing our beloved home. We were strangers to you and you took Astrid's word that we were worth knowing. You blended in effortlessly and when the terrible tragedy of the fire occurred you discreetly stayed in the background and let us grieve. It must have been a really difficult time for you, but you never let us down. You could have left, returned to the States, but instead you stayed and showed us great kindness, bringing us to Dublin for that lovely holiday in the Shelbourne Hotel. I thank you so much for those special times.

Your investment in the Folly saved our home and although I know it was a business arrangement, I also know it meant more than that to you. You came to live among us, you became our dear and most valued friend. There is nothing I can do, or give to you to show my love and esteem, except to wish you a happy life always in The Folly. I hope you never leave and that one day, many years from now, that you too will make the woodland in The Folly garden, your final resting place.

Goodbye my lovely friend,
with all my love,
Lizzy

Edie stood up and giving each of her friends a hug, said quietly: 'Lizzy speaks for both of us. Thank you all for your friendship.'

The evening passed peacefully. The others came in from the cottages to join them and Arthur arrived from the village. Jayne decided to stay at the hotel with Edie for a few nights to keep her company and Beatrice and Magdalena also took over a guest suite. They had no power in the house. Tony and Peter decided not to move.

'We've lots of candles, the range for heating and cooking and actually, I think it will be rather cosy in the cottage,' Peter enthused, squeezing Tony's hand. 'I think we'll enjoy sitting out the storm in the stable yard.'

Jayne smiled thinking of Lizzy's tight lipped disapproval of the boys' open display of affection for one another. The Thorns were also self-sufficient and although they stayed late in the bar enjoying the wine and company they made their way home.

Before this, Edie spoke to the group. 'While we are all gathered here, I would like to make a proposal. Lizzy requested that her ashes be spread, along with Dorothea's, in the garden. I hope you agree that we should repeat the ceremony we held at the time of Dorothea's death. I would like to hold it in the garden followed by a party in the house for all our friends and neighbours. What do you think? Let's celebrate Lizzy's life. That's what she wanted.'

There was a general murmur of agreement and then Magdalena voiced total support for Edie's suggestion.

'What a wonderful idea. When would you like to hold the party, Edie?'

At this, Edie hesitated and with a slight break in her voice, replied: 'You may think I'm a sentimental old fool but I would like to keep Lizzy's ashes in the house for a few weeks before spreading them in the garden.'

Everyone agreed. 'Let's hold the ceremony in late summer. That's a lovely time of year. The garden will be in its full glory and who knows the sun might shine.'

She again looked pensive and sitting down, signalled to Jayne and Arthur to join them.

'There is something else I need to discuss with you. We should contact Louisa, shouldn't we? After all, regardless of past events, she is our sister.'

Leaving the others to discuss Louisa, Eve Langton slipped away and made her way to her apartment. Retrieving the letter from her bag, she reread it for about the tenth time that day. It arrived earlier, just as she was about to leave for the funeral. It was disturbing and plunged her back into the nightmare of her past. All the emotions became confused: anger mixed with remorse, guilt mixed with shame, relief with anxiety.

Should she now share her secret with these people who had become her friends, who shouldn't judge her for what was not her fault? It was the first time in years she felt safe, safe in the knowledge that she did have a life of her own. She had people in her life who loved her. She was not alone. Could she ever feel complete in this new life if she did not let her friends know the true story, the real story.

Eve arrived back in the bar but the others hardly noticed her absence, being so absorbed in discussing whether Edie should contact Louisa.

Magdalena made it perfectly clear she was not convinced contacting Louisa was a good idea. She made no apology for saying this, like the other friends, she felt very protective towards Edie.

'I appreciate she is your sister, Edie but do you think she will want to know about Lizzy, or will she just hurt you again? She is an extremely selfish woman as we learned the hard way.'

No one wanted to say too much for fear of upsetting her.

'Perhaps the best plan is to follow your heart, Edie,' Jayne added and said no more.

Arthur had never met Louisa but the association with her son had ended in sadness for his daughter so he was more inclined to agree with Magdalena and let sleeping dogs lie.

Edie interjected: 'I don't believe she will do anything about it should I contact her, so provided I can handle rejection and being ignored, it would do no harm to let her know what's going on.'

Beatrice had never met Louisa either but heard the stories about her. She didn't want to offer an opinion so laughed and said: 'I hope you don't mind me saying this but poor Lizzy would turn in her grave if she thought Louisa was in any way involved. She was unforgiving and from what I hear, she had a point.'

Edie replied: 'Let's sleep on it and I'll make a decision in the morning.'

Eve in the meantime slipped up to the bar and ordered a brandy for Dutch courage. Offering everyone a drink, she sat down and said there was something she wanted to tell them.

'You have all become very dear to me and I trust you. On many occasions I wanted to share the secrets of my past with you, especially you Jayne, when you were nursing me through that dreadful flu. I will never be free until I confide in you as my friends. Secrets separate people. They create barriers, so here goes.'

She told them she received a letter that morning telling her of her husband's death. This was a major surprise as none of them knew Eve was married. No one interrupted, this seemed only the beginning of a much longer saga. Eve told them of the dreadful crimes her husband committed, the years when she lived in ignorance of his embezzlement of people's hard earned money, of the hardship and misery he had caused. Telling them gave her great relief.

'Undoubtedly the worst part of the whole dreadful business was that he murdered a policeman and received the death sentence with many years on death row. So sordid and sinister. I'm really sorry to speak about it tonight on this sad occasion, but the time seems right. It's over now. He died of a heart attack. Just one person in the prison service is privy to my new life, my whereabouts. He sent me the news. I feel liberated. I want to start again, make this a new chapter in my life.' She said no more.

There was a stunned silence. Then Arthur said: 'Eve, I'm sure everyone here agrees you are a brave woman and we wish you happiness in your new life among us here in Crannagh.'

Eve experienced a wonderful sense of belonging as each one gave her a reassuring hug, letting her know the past was now well behind her.

Chapter 43

The weeks following Lizzy's funeral were relatively uneventful. The long, bright summer days attracted tourists to the area, the restaurant and bar were busy, many visitors on fine days choosing to eat outdoors in the garden or have their drinks in the beer garden. Finn's Folly was a hive of activity. Business was booming.

The garden produced a fine crop of vegetables, fruits and herbs under the dedicated care of Isaac and Matilda. The products made by Mary, Peter and Tony became even better and they won many awards during that summer at food fairs in the vicinity. The cream of the crop was winning first place at the Dungarvan Food Festival, an event rated highly among food and wine buffs of Ireland's culinary community. This award also gave them automatic entry into the most prestigious food fair, held in Dublin later in the year.

Working with Chef Ricardo and the local historic society, they decided to publish a book of recipes, using their own and local produce, along with photographs old and new of The Folly and anecdotes about the old house, the Finn family and the surrounding area. Edie was particularly excited about this project, wishing Lizzy could be there to see it. She threw herself into researching the family and the house and dug up all sorts of old photographs and documents. It helped greatly in her grief, as she felt close to her sister and often laughed and cried at the memories it brought to mind. Jayne was always on hand to help, as was Eve.

Inspired by this project and seeing how it was helping Edie, Eve came up with a brainwave of her own. Since her revelations to her friends about her life, she had a renewed energy and decided to pursue one of her oldest hobbies, photography. Saying nothing about her mission, she headed off to Dublin and bought a state of the art piece of equipment. For several days she wandered around the area, taking numerous photographs and when satisfied she still had the talent and ability of her younger years, she showed her work to the others. They were impressed at the wonderful artistic talent she had and without delay asked her to do the photography for the new book.

Sarah, meanwhile, took leave of absence from work for a couple of months, to move into Forest Cottage. While there Dr Mangan asked her to help him in his surgery from time to time. The work was interesting and a way to meet the locals. She was surprised but pleased when he asked if she would consider a permanent position.

'I can't offer you the money you're used to from the hospital, Sarah,' he told her, 'but your hours would be shorter and very sociable, no night duty or weekends.'

It was so tempting that weighing up the pros and cons and chatting with Jayne, within 24 hours she accepted the offer.

'Ever since you moved here Jayne, I've had this longing to do the same. It's a special place, isn't it?'

Jayne agreed wholeheartedly, because even though she had experienced tough times recently, she seemed to cope much better than before and was also much happier. The arrangement with Jack was a bit tricky, but it was working out, with a bit of effort and help from her friends. James was very happy, loving both homes and families and that was what mattered.

Outwardly Jayne was coping well since Lizzy's death. She missed her dreadfully but her own grief was sidelined by her efforts to keep up Edie's spirits. She also missed Marcus dreadfully and had practically no social life. She didn't want to make a fool of herself, because in her heart, she believed she would soon have to face up to the awful truth that Marcus was not coming back to her. Edie had not heard from

Louisa since contacting her about Lizzy's death. This didn't surprise anyone, especially Edie, but it made Jayne more angry with her.

'She could at least have acknowledged Edie's letter,' she complained to Sarah. 'Good manners cost nothing.'

'I'd say she's making it clear she wants nothing to do with any of us here in Ireland. Well, off with her I say, she's not worth worrying about.' As usual Sarah hit the nail on the head but Louisa's bad behaviour still niggled away at Jayne.

The last time she spoke to Abigail she told her Marcus had left Cape Town and had gone for a long stay in some out of the way place in the Eastern Cape. Abigail had no contact details for him and didn't expect him back any time soon. It seemed he had no desire to have any contact with her or with anyone else in Crannagh. Jayne was distraught but kept her feelings to herself.

Chapter 44

Some weeks later on a dreary afternoon in September, Jayne walked from the stable yard to the hotel. She was going to The Olivia Suite to help Edie prepare for the spreading of Lizzy's ashes. The busy summer season was drawing to a close, as the days became shorter and summer holidays came to an end. Sandra O'Leary closed the hotel to non-residents for the occasion. All neighbours and friends were invited along with the residents. Some of the regular holiday guests, who became friends with Lizzy over the years, also returned as a mark of respect.

Jayne found Edie daydreaming in the bay window holding Lizzy's ashes as she looked down over the woodland where Dorothea was laid to rest. She looked up as Jayne came into the room.

'Oh Jayne, it's you. I was away in a world of my own. This is a rather strange day, isn't it, saying goodbye to Lizzy. She was always such a character, never spoke anything but the truth, with no time for nonsense.'

She hesitated as she went off into a reverie again.

'You know Jayne, it would have broken her heart had we lost The Folly. It came so close, didn't it? Really, thanks to Astrid and Magdalena and, of course, Marcus, it was saved and what a wonderful reinvention they created. Who would have thought this old place could bring so much happiness to so many people?'

Jayne was setting out Edie's outfit for the day. She chose a bright primrose dress and jacket, as Edie decided everyone should dress for a celebration.

'We wore our funeral clothes on the day of the cremation; today we must deck out in our finery.'

Jayne was looking very pretty and elegant in a delicate shade of blue, complementing her dark hair and tanned skin. Recently Edie had been concerned about Jayne. She sensed there was a sadness about her and she looked fragile, having lost a lot of weight since coming back from South Africa. She knew Jayne was happy at The Folly, now part owner of the business and owning her cottage which came with her inheritance, so she was really secure. James was a healthy, happy boy and although the situation with Jack wasn't perfect, it worked fairly well. Having Arthur back in her life brought her wonderful happiness and with him came her lovely brother and sister but no one could fill the empty space left by Marcus. Edie was wise enough to see that but was sad she could do nothing about it.

But she decided to speak to her now, having avoided the subject for a long time so as not to upset her. Patting the window seat beside her, she invited Jayne to sit next to her and took her hand.

'Jayne, you do know how special you are to me, as you were to Lizzy? Will you be able to move on with your life after Marcus? I know you loved him, but I fear you'll let your young life drift away. You are a beautiful young woman and you deserve the happiness a good relationship will bring to you.'

Jayne nodded slowly and looking into Edie's eyes, told her with complete honesty she was still in love with Marcus and for now would rather be alone if she couldn't be with him.

Downstairs, meanwhile, the guests gathered in the drawing room for refreshments before heading down the garden to the woodland. Everyone followed Edie's wishes and the room was full of bright colours, lending cheer to the gloomy day. When they were ready to leave with the ashes, Jayne took James by the hand, escorting Edie who led the little procession through The Folly garden to the woodland. The ceremony was short but poignant, Edie saying a special few words of farewell to her beloved sister. As she spoke, Jayne looked around at all the friends gathered. She wondered what was going through their minds standing in the garden of the beautiful house, the house that was now their home. She wondered what happiness came into dreary lives, what friendships into lonely lives and what love to those who grew to believe they were destined to live out their lives alone. The Folly, Finn's Folly, rose from the ashes and became the centre of so many worlds.

As the strains of Lizzy's favourite song, 'Oh Danny Boy', reverberated through the autumn air, the poignant lines brought tears to their eyes as the guests joined in the chorus.

But come ye back when summer's in the meadow,
Or when the valley's hushed and white with snow,
'Tis I'll be here, in sunshine or in shadow,
Oh Danny boy, oh Danny boy, I love you so!

Just then the clouds parted, the sun shone brightly and the garden became alive with colour and feelings of joy.

Jayne stood with James, tears trickling down her face and at that very moment a large hand was laid gently on her shoulder and a familiar voice whispered in her ear.

'It's me, Jayne, I'm back, back where I belong, with you. Is that alright?'

Startled, she turned around, to find Marcus, looking into her eyes, tall, slim, tanned and healthy. Her heart skipped a beat. Without uttering a word, but remembering Lizzy's remark that one day the sun would shine for her again, looking up at the blue sky and the bright sunshine, she took his hand in hers, squeezing it and resolved never to let him go again.

THE END